W9-BAU-330

Flawless

Flawless

LARA CHAPMAN

BLOOMSBURY

NEW YORK BERLIN LONDON SYDNEY

First published in the United States of America in May 2011
by Bloomsbury Books for Young Readers
www.bloomsburyteens.com

For information about permission to reproduce selections from this book, write to
Permissions, Bloomsbury BFYR, 175 Fifth Avenue, New York, New York 10010

Library of Congress Cataloging-in-Publication Data
Chapman, Lara.
Flawless / by Lara Chapman. — 1st U.S. ed.
p.   cm.
Summary: In this modern take on the Cyrano story, brilliant and witty high school student
Sarah Burke, who is cursed with an enormous nose, helps her beautiful best friend try to win
the heart of a handsome and smart new student, even though Sarah wants him for herself.
ISBN 978-1-59990-596-9 (paperback) • ISBN 978-1-59990-631-7 (hardcover)
[1. Beauty, Personal—Fiction. 2. Friendship—Fiction. 3. Self-confidence—Fiction.
4. High schools—Fiction. 5. Schools—Fiction.] I. Title.
PZ7.C3715Fl 2011   [Fic]—dc22   2010049102

Book design by Donna Mark
Typeset by Westchester Book Composition
Printed in the U.S.A. by Quad/Graphics, Fairfield, Pennsylvania
2 4 6 8 10 9 7 5 3 1 (paperback)
2 4 6 8 10 9 7 5 3 1 (hardcover)

All papers used by Bloomsbury Publishing, Inc., are natural, recyclable products
made from wood grown in well-managed forests. The manufacturing processes
conform to the environmental regulations of the country of origin.

For Caleb & Laney . . .
Love redefined

Flawless

There is nothing so agonizing to the fine skin of
vanity as the application of a rough truth.
—EDWARD BULWER-LYTTON

Chapter One

I love the first day of school. There's nothing like a new start. New clothes, new classes, new goals. And maybe, just maybe, the possibility of meeting a new guy.

Especially when you're a senior in high school.

With a final glance at the ensemble I've put together for my last first day of high school and a mental kiss to the hair gods for my stunning naturally blond, wavy hair, I close my bedroom door, then dance downstairs.

Where I slam headfirst into reality.

Next to my *"You Are Special Today"* plate, a tradition my mother started on my first day of kindergarten, polished silverware sits on top of a rhinoplasty brochure.

No napkin. Just the brochure.

I ignore my mother's watchful eyes. "Real subtle, Mom." I move the silverware, then flick the glossy trifold with the tip of my finger, scoring a beautiful two-pointer as it lands in the silver-and-black trash can.

I hate the word "rhinoplasty." How can you not think of a disgusting two-ton mammal when you hear that word?

Just call it what it is—a nose job.

Spatula in one hand, Mom pops the other hand onto her hip. "Just a suggestion, Sarah."

"Yet still offensive. Couldn't you have waited until, like, the *second* day of school to start in on me?" I stab the tasteless egg-white omelet on my plate, wishing there were some crispy strips of bacon sitting next to it. It's hard to believe I was actually born to this health-conscious, runway-worthy woman. Being a Burke can be a serious pain in the butt.

"I only want what's best for you. Now that you're a senior, you're old enough to make those changes we've always talked about."

I drop the fork to my plate. "Not *we*, Mom. *You*. I don't recall asking for the privilege of having some wacko chop away at the nose *you* gave me. Just because you changed yours when you were eighteen doesn't mean I have to."

The honest truth is that I never would have requested this particular nose, but I've spent seventeen years learning to accept it.

"Sarah . . ." Mom stares at me, the wheels of her brain churning at top speed while her own omelet sizzles in the abandoned skillet. She doesn't have to say what I know she's thinking. *How in the world will Beth Burke's daughter ever follow in her news-broadcasting footsteps with a honker the size of a Buick?*

I nod at the smoking skillet. "You're burning."

Cursing under her breath, she drops the tiny pan into the sink just as a car horn beeps from the curb, officially signaling the end to our fight like a bell at the end of a boxing match.

Thank God she's on time. For once.

"That's Kristen." I swallow the last of my orange juice before leaning across the expansive polished granite counter that serves as our breakfast table to kiss Mom on the cheek. "Have a good day, Mom."

"But you didn't eat anything."

"No time. See you tonight." Grabbing my backpack, I walk out the door with one final look back just in time to see her fishing out the brochure I'd tossed in the trash.

+ + +

Mom and I moved to Houston when I was in third grade. When I was young and foolish and thought my face was "special." When I thought it was cool to be different.

I met Kristen Gallagher on my first day of school. A boy named Beaver Collins called me Pinocchio and Kristen thumped him on the ear in my defense. We've been best friends ever since.

I slide into Kristen's bright yellow Mustang, Fergie blasting from the radio. A huge Walmart bag of school supplies and a zebra-striped backpack with the tags still attached are strewn over the backseat.

"You're killing me with this." I reach in the back and grab her supplies, knowing that if I don't, she'll walk into school completely unorganized. Just the thought of it makes me cringe. And she knows it.

With one last smack of her freshly glossed lips, she closes the visor mirror, then turns and smiles, affording me the full view of her spectacular face, and for an instant, a moment, a nanosecond, I hate her. Every single feature on her face is the right shape and textbook proportionate.

"Now why should I bother with that? You're just going to tell me I did it wrong and redo it for me anyway." She flashes her dimples—yet one more facial feature that adds to her good looks—and puts the car into drive.

The truth is she's right. Despite my tendency to be a tiny bit compulsive, especially when it comes to organization, she doesn't give me any grief. Instead, she takes it in stride, laughing at my insane need to control things. Not that she hasn't totally benefited from my downfall. I've been keeping her on track for as long as I've known her.

In return, she's my personal cheerleader. The one who keeps telling me my face has character. That I'm destined for greatness with a face like this. Although I doubt my face is going to make me famous. More like infamous.

"How's Mom this morning?" Kristen knows the tragic history of first-day events with my mom. Like the first day of my freshman year when she brought the news cameras to follow me around school, chronicling "The Life of Today's High School Student" for an in-depth news exposé. Not exactly the innocuous beginning I'd had planned for myself.

"For breakfast, she served me an egg-white omelet with a nose-job sales pitch."

Kristen shakes her head. "I swear, they should make adults pass some sort of test before they're allowed to have children. I don't know why she even bothers. As far as I'm concerned, you're perfect just the way you are."

"That's why I love you," I tell her.

By the time we screech to a halt in front of Northwest High School, Kristen's supplies are organized and my ears are ringing, still echoing the Nickelback lyrics blessedly cut off when she yanked the key out of the ignition. Don't get me wrong, I love Nickelback as much as the next person, but not at a pulse-pounding volume at seven thirty in the morning.

"Ready?" she asks, hand on the door handle.

"Born ready," I say, repeating the same thing we've said to each other every day for the last four years.

The first day of school is really a double-edged sword for someone like me. Yes, I love "first days," but it also means I have to meet a sea of new faces in the hallways, freshmen who've never seen me before.

Or more accurately, freshmen who've never seen my *nose* before.

Shoulder to shoulder, we hike the twenty-one steps that lead to the front doors of our high school, waving at friends, and handing out smiles and shout-outs like presidential candidates. If someone had a baby, we'd kiss it.

And then it happens. The inevitable. The one thing I dread on the first day of school. It starts with a whisper that becomes a giggle, then spreads into a small rumble of conversation. By the time we've reached the top of the stairs, my heart is thudding in my chest like a jackhammer.

"Here we go," Kristen says with a conspiratorial wink. I follow her lead when she stops and turns to face the gawking students lining the stairs.

"Everyone take cover! She's gonna blow!" Kristen shouts, covering her head dramatically.

Immediately, every visible person drops to the ground, covering their heads. Everyone except Mr. McGinty, the school counselor who's been trying to be my best friend the entire time I've been a student at Northwest. I've always ignored him, convinced he's trying to use me as a case study for some psychology journal. But now he's standing at the base of the stairs, smiling up at me with a goofy thumbs-up held high above his head. I can't help but smile back.

Kristen lifts her hand and high-fives me.

"Kidding," I sing out right on cue, then give a small wave to the shocked students. As we walk into the building, I hear the melody of students laughing and clapping behind us.

✦ ✦ ✦

Kristen and I have only three classes together: journalism, choir, and gym. Despite my best efforts to prove to her the importance of advanced-placement courses on college acceptance, she's content with an average GPA. While I'm taking Advanced Physics this year, she'll be soaking up Intro to Geology. While I'm in a dual-credit economics course, she'll be manning the school store.

When I walk into journalism for third period, Kristen waves to me from our usual spot in the back right corner of the classroom. She's got her feet stretched out on the seat in front of her in an attempt to keep others out of her space. I love her, but she can be a snob like that.

I slip into my seat beside her, the cold, aged plastic scraping the back of my jeans. God, I hate school chairs. "How have your classes been?" I ask.

"Good, I guess. It's lining up to be an easy coast year." Kristen slides her hand in a rolling-with-the-flow kind of motion.

"And you're okay with that?" I don't know why I even ask when I already know the answer.

"Are you kidding? It's what I've been praying for. This year is all about having some fun. When are you going to take a break and just let loose? Go a little crazy?"

"After college." I have it all planned. After I graduate, land my dream job, and get an apartment in Dallas, I'll let loose, just be wild and crazy. But until then, I work my ass off.

At precisely that moment, the balance of my orderly life crumbles like a house of cards.

The once-buzzing classroom freezes. Standing in the doorway is the hottest guy I've ever laid eyes on. Golden brown hair cut just short enough to be stylish and a body I've only seen on television. Honest to God, the room has fallen dead silent while he looks at his schedule and compares it to the number on the door.

You can almost hear every girl's thoughts.

Please be in this class.

Please take me to the prom.

Please marry me.

And every guy's thoughts.

I hope he plays football.

I hope he plays baseball.

I hope he's got a girlfriend and leaves mine alone.

When he looks up and finds everyone staring, he glances behind himself to see what they're looking at. Realizing he's the center of attention, he smiles, upping the charm of his rugged good looks when his slightly imperfect teeth are revealed. I give an audible sigh of appreciation.

Kristen reaches out, grabs my hand, squeezes it, and whispers, "I'm in love."

I know how she feels. It's the same thing every single girl in the class is feeling, including me.

Then all at once, the spell is broken and the class is back in action. A group of girls from the drill team wave to get his attention, but none of them stand a chance against Kristen.

Sliding from her seat, she stands, flicks her straightened blond hair over her shoulder, and walks her tan, long legs to the door. Without a word, they proceed, arm in arm like they've just been nominated homecoming king and queen, back to the vacant seat in front of her.

"Welcome to Northwest," she purrs, her voice resonating with a hoarseness I've never heard. When'd she learn that? "I'm Kristen Gallagher, and this is my best friend, Sarah Burke."

He nods back at Kristen, a smitten grin spread across his face. "Rockford Conway. Everyone calls me Rock."

I instantaneously think how much I'd love to be stuck between Rock and a hard place when he turns to acknowledge me. His gaze stops at the most obvious spot on my face.

Not my killer blue eyes.

Not my pouty lips.

Not even my precious little chin.

His eyes lock dead center on my face.

On my nose.

As he studies me silently, fire burns its way up my cheeks. There can be no doubt he's taking in the beaklike quality I've learned to appreciate. Well, "appreciate" might be a stretch. You learn to appreciate fine art or classical music, and my nose is a long way from those things. I guess you could say I've learned to tolerate my nose.

Until now.

At this very second, I'd give anything to be sitting in the doctor's office, taking "before" pictures and scheduling the blasted rhinoplasty.

"Nice to meet you, Rock," I say, extending my hand for a shake. Anything to break the intensity of his eyes on my ginormous flaw.

As if shaking himself awake from a bad dream, he forces his eyes to lock with mine and he smiles. You know how you can just tell you're going to hit it off with someone when you first meet? That's how I feel the second we make eye contact. There's a tenderness, an understanding in his eyes that makes me feel like I already know him. He's actually looking me *in the eyes* and I get the feeling he's trying to send me some sort of telepathic "You're uniquely beautiful" message. Of course, I'm no psychic. That's just my interpretation.

His hand totally covers my own, sending a jolt of awareness through my body and landing squarely in my stomach like a basketball. Our school has like a thousand students, and you can assume that half of those students are boys. But not once have I ever been so taken with a guy. Ever. It nearly kills me to break the contact with him when he pulls his hand away. I do my best to look unaffected as the jackhammer works overtime in my chest.

"Where are you from, Rock?" Kristen leans forward, effortlessly executing a move she calls the "lean and look." You lean in, he looks at your chest. I'm silently satisfied when he doesn't do his part, but keeps his eyes on her face.

"Atlanta."

I'm frozen in place, watching Kristen keep his attention while I sit speechless, which, in and of itself, is something of a rarity. For once, I wish I'd listened to Kristen when she was telling me about the romance magazine article on how to get a guy's attention.

Speak, damn it, speak!

"A southern boy," Kristen drawls, leaning even closer so that she—and her boobs—are mere inches from his face.

"When did you move here, Rock?" I finally get the words out, barely recognizing my voice, which sounds squeaky and prepubescent to my own ears. Great. This is so typical. Kristen sounds like a lioness and I sound like Kermit the Frog with a head cold.

"A couple of weeks ago. My dad's an oil and gas attorney. In that industry, all roads lead to Houston, right?"

"Absolutely," Kristen answers.

But a funny thing happens. Instead of turning his attention

to the hard-to-ignore wet dream nearly sitting on top of him, Rock's looking at me.

As if Kristen hadn't said anything.

As if what I have to say matters.

As if . . .

My thoughts are callously interrupted by Mrs. Freel's scratchy voice, well earned from years of screaming at out-of-control students. "Welcome back to school, kids. Let's get started."

Kristen falls back into her seat, exhaling for the first time in five minutes.

Rock smiles and gives me one last lingering look before facing the front of the classroom, as if to say we'd continue our conversation later.

Right.

As if.

The absence of flaw in beauty is itself a flaw.
—HAVELOCK ELLIS

Chapter Two

I spend the entire class period memorizing the back of Rock's head, obsessively overanalyzing that last little look, convincing myself it was all in my imagination.

When the bell rings at the end of class, he stretches back, raising his arms above his head. Even from where I'm sitting, I can see the bottom of his T-shirt rise just above his hip-hugging jeans. I'm struck speechless when the muscles in his arms bulge under the thin weight of his plain gray T-shirt.

An Adonis has arrived and I'm here to worship him.

"So what'd you think, Rock?" Kristen purrs . . . again. I can't decide if I want to slap some sense into her or copy her every move.

"Stimulating," he says, turning to give her a grin that I totally wish was meant for me.

"You took the words right out of my mouth," she answers back with a come-and-get-me grin. I'm mesmerized by the sex-kitten transformation taking place in front of my eyes. Kristen's had lots of dates and even a few serious boyfriends, but she's always been . . . well, Kristen. Funny, a little ditzy, and raring for a good time. Not sexy, smitten, and shameless.

Rock pulls a folded schedule out of his back pocket as he stands. "Fourth period, American lit. Where are you girls headed?"

There *is* a God and he likes me. He really, *really* likes me.

"Same as you," I say, a smile spreading across my face. "I'll show you the way."

"Get out!" Kristen narrows her eyes at me, like I created his schedule. Like I could ever compete with her.

"It's okay," Rock says, misinterpreting her minitantrum as sympathy. He leans in close to Kristen's ear and whispers loud enough for me to hear. "Don't tell anyone, but I actually like literature."

He's gorgeous *and* he likes literature?

Okay, it's official. I might be in love.

"Eww." Kristen turns up her nose as if someone just told her they like eating sheep eyes for breakfast. "Seriously?"

" 'Fraid so," he says, shaking his head in mock embarrassment. He turns his attention to me with a wink. "Ready?" he asks.

Maybe it's out of habit from answering Kristen's exact same question for four years, but I answer without thinking. "Born ready."

+ + +

If you think your life can't change in the blink of an eye, you're wrong.

If you think people don't care who you're friends with, you're wrong.

If you think walking down the halls of your high school with someone like Rock doesn't change the way people look at you, you're wrong.

Dead wrong.

If I were alone, the stroll to my next class would be a repeat of every other first day, where I would walk quickly and pretend to ignore the occasional whisper and stare. Instead, Rock and I get the old double take, heads whipping, mouths gaping, minds reeling.

I know what they're thinking. *Who's that hottie? And what's he doing with* her? It's not like I blame them; I'm wondering the same thing.

"Need to stop at your locker?" Rock's voice forces me to pull my attention from the spectators lining the expansive hallway leading to Mr. Jacobi's musty classroom.

"That's okay. I can put my things up after lit."

"You're the boss," he says, giving me a goofy little salute. Who knew goofy could be sexy?

"Here we are," I announce inanely, like he couldn't figure that out by reading the big banner stretching across the top of Jacobi's door that reads LIT'S FOR LEADERS.

Rock places his fingertips on my back just above my waistband, sending my senses into overdrive. "After you," he whispers near my ear.

I fight the habit of sitting in the front row and take a seat in the middle of the classroom. When Rock takes the seat behind me, I mentally kick myself, wishing I'd sat behind him so I could spend another class period studying him unnoticed.

I turn in my seat to face Rock, whose eyes are taking in the room around him. The posters on the wall are yellowed, either from age or Jacobi's illegal pipe smoking in the classroom. There are stacks of books lining every square inch of wall space, some blocking bookcases that hold even more books.

"Wow," Rock says. "I thought *I* had a lot of books, but I'm an amateur compared to this guy."

I follow Rock's eyes around the room. "I know. He's like a total lit freak. Everything he says is loaded with meaning and based on years of study. I think he's got three master's degrees or something. He's a little weird, but I like him."

Rock's attention shoots back to me, the smile on his face so breathtaking I nearly pant. "Weird, huh? I'm kind of into weird, too."

Mr. Jacobi enters the room, the sweet smell of his pipe tobacco filling the room. He drops his tattered leather book bag onto his desk ceremoniously, silencing the classroom.

"Our theme for this year," he booms, "is what rules every decision we make as adults. It's the root of every poem ever written. Anyone want to take a guess?"

"Pride," Jeremy Pickett squeaks. Poor little guy still looks and sounds like he's in eighth grade.

15

Jacobi shakes his head.

"Greed," another student calls out.

"Jealousy," says another.

"Warmer," Jacobi says.

Rock's voice rumbles over my head. "Love."

With one finger on his nose, Jacobi points to Rock with his other hand. "Bingo." Jacobi walks to Rock and extends his hand. "I don't believe we've met. Arthur Jacobi."

"Rock Conway." Rock slides out of his seat to stand, and the two shake like esteemed colleagues, not like teacher and student.

"Welcome to Northwest, Mr. Conway. It's good to have you." When Jacobi walks to the front of the classroom, I stretch my hand behind my back and Rock slaps it in a high five. It's so natural, like we've done it a hundred times.

Sitting on his decrepit desk, Jacobi addresses the packed classroom. "For the next 186 days of school, we'll focus on love. Love of money, love of material things, love of self, love of others. Love that destroys and unites nations. Love that creates families and ruins relationships. It's the most powerful human emotion, driving us to sacrifice almost anything to get it and, once we have it, keep it. It's driven men to murder, to war, and to suicide. It's more than roses and candy; it's a living part of who we are, what we believe in. It can create and obliterate our identity. With love, you can do anything. Without it, you're nothing." Fist in the air, à la *Braveheart*, he pounds out his final words. "Love is power!"

I'm watching Jacobi and wondering how love has played a

part in his life. What has he done for love? It's hard to imagine Jacobi driven to violence in the name of love.

More to the point, what would *I* do for love? I mean, it's not like I've ever been close to being in love, but if I was, what would I do to keep it? Would I sacrifice my brand-new BCBG boots? The college scholarships I've worked so hard to earn?

"It's all about love, folks. You can see it right here in the halls of Northwest. It's why girls wear what they wear each day and why boys fight for their place on the top of the heap. Everyone's looking for it." Jacobi raises his right eyebrow in question as he glances across the faces looking back at him intently. "Aren't you?"

Silent affirmations charge the air and Jacobi nods. "I rest my case," he says. "Now, let's get down to business."

When the bell rings forty minutes later, we have a four-page syllabus and two books: *The Scarlet Letter* by Nathaniel Hawthorne and *The Complete Poems of Emily Dickinson*.

Arms loaded down, Rock and I are stopped by Jacobi on our way to the door. "Welcome back, Miss Burke," he says, his familiar smile lighting his face.

"Yourself," I say, enjoying the surge of excitement at starting the year with such an awesome lit topic. I mean, who doesn't want to talk about love?

"And you, Mr. Conway. I'm looking forward to working with you this year. The fact that you've made friends with Sarah speaks highly of your character."

I feel the telltale warmth spread across my cheeks; I'm simultaneously flattered and embarrassed.

17

Rock chuckles deeply. "Thank you."

"See you tomorrow," Jacobi says, dismissing us with a wave of his hand as he sits in the threadbare office chair behind his desk.

✦ ✦ ✦

"Need me to show you where the cafeteria is?" I ask once we're outside Jacobi's room.

"Actually, I was hoping you'd let me eat with you. There's nothing worse than eating by yourself in a new school."

I squelch the cheer rising in my chest. "Sure. I need to run by my locker first."

"Lead the way," he says casually.

Walking through the crowded hallway, I'm stunned at my good fortune of meeting Rock. It's like we've known each other for years.

When we reach my locker, I throw it open and toss my books inside.

"Mind if I leave mine in here, too? My locker's on the bottom and it's nearly impossible for me to get to."

"Of course," I say, the frog settling back in my throat. Heat spreads across my chest when he reaches around me and places the books on top of my own. It seems so . . . intimate. And, God help me, I love it.

At Northwest, all the seniors have lunch at the same time, so the cafeteria's really crowded, really loud. Off-campus lunches were stripped from us last year when a group of cheerleaders got drunk at lunch and had a wreck on their way back to school. Since then, we've been forced to eat at school, all 250 seniors at one time.

"I'm headed for the salad bar, but there's a grill over there," I say, pointing to the red-and-white-canopied corner of the cafeteria with a long line of guys patiently waiting for their double cheeseburgers and chili cheese fries.

"Salad's good for me, too," he says.

"Okay, then follow me." As we get in line at the salad bar, Kristen breezes through the door and waves when she spots us.

My stomach drops at the sight of her. I'm not quite ready to share Rock so soon, not to mention the backseat I'll be taking to Kristen.

Ignoring the glares of everyone in line behind us, she nestles herself between me and Rock. "Miss me?" she chirps.

"You have no idea," I mumble.

"Did you make it through Jacobi's class?" she asks Rock, rolling her eyes. "I swear I nearly killed myself the week I was in there last year. It was brutal. I finally begged my way out."

Rock's easy laugh slips from his lips. "It was actually pretty interesting."

Kristen's eyes dart from my face to Rock's. "What's his depressing life-altering theme this year? War? Famine? Poverty?"

I'm quick to answer, Jacobi's inspiring words still rambling around in my head. "Love."

Kristen shakes her head in pity. "Poor things," she says.

"Don't feel sorry for us," Rock says, his dark brown eyes glancing at me over Kristen's head. "I think it's going to be my favorite class." Our gazes lock for just a second, and it's like we're sharing something. I don't know what it is, but I swear something is there.

"For real?" Kristen asks, dazzling blues wide in surprise.

"Absolutely. What's not to love?" Rock gently nudges Kristen forward in line.

I can tell by the look on Kristen's face that she's scrambling for the right words. "Well, I'm just saying that love is a pretty lame theme, even for Jacobi."

"So what's your favorite thing to read, Kristen?" he asks.

"I'm more of a magazine reader."

"Oh yeah? What kind of magazines?" Rock's interest is totally genuine and I can hardly wait to see his reaction to the answer I know is coming.

"*Teen Vogue, Cosmo.* That kind of thing."

Rock winks at Kristen in a way that makes me want to scream. It's already happening. "Well, all that reading has paid off, gorgeous. You are, hands down, the most stunning girl in this entire building."

And just like that, I'm back to where I've always been.

In Kristen's shadow.

*I never saw an ugly thing in my life; for let the
form of an object be what it may—light, shade,
and perspective will always make it beautiful.*
—JOHN CONSTABLE

Chapter Three

After school, Kristen and I head to Sandy's Nails. Most of our friends get their nails and feet done before school starts, but going after the first day of school has become a tradition. The first year we came to Sandy's the week before school started; we had to wait an hour and then got nothing more than a glorified footbath with a polish change. Coming after school starts changed everything. We get to relax and gossip and the salon is practically deserted, which means Sandy and her sister, Nan, give us a lot of attention.

We sit side by side in superdeluxe massaging pedicure chairs, then drop our bare feet into the soapy hot water. How is it that a spa pedicure can make everything better?

Kristen leans her head sideways to look at me. "Give me the update on your college apps."

I close my eyes, visualizing the list of colleges I've applied to, ranked in order. "I should hear back from the University of Texas by late fall."

"And the others?" Kristen knows my first choice is the University of Texas. It's close to home and has a kick-ass communications program.

I shrug. "Got my acceptance to Rice in July, but I really don't want to stay in Houston."

Kristen nods. "No way am I staying here, either."

"Still set on Texas State?" Texas State has long been known as a party college, but a good one nonetheless. It could be a great fit for Kristen, but I can't imagine living an hour away from her.

"Yep," she says, grinning. "I can't wait to get out on my own."

"On your own?" I say, laughing.

"Yes, on my own."

"As in supporting yourself?"

Kristen scowls. "Okay, Debbie Downer. That'll be enough."

"Seriously. Are you going to get a job?"

She nods, eyes closed as Nan rubs her feet.

"Any thoughts about where?"

"Dr. Randall at the animal shelter said he'd put in a couple of phone calls for me as it got closer to next fall. Hopefully I can land something at a vet clinic or shelter there."

"That's awesome, Kris!" I stare at my friend, whose eyes are still closed, a small grin on her lips. She'd never told me she planned to work when she moved. I'm totally impressed.

She opens her eyes just a sliver. "Bet you've already got a job lined up, don't you?"

I smile back at her. "Not yet."

"But you will. That's just how you work."

A part of me feels like I should apologize for not being more spontaneous, but she's right. That's not who I am. "Fail to plan . . ."

"Plan to fail," she completes. "God, you're predictable."

Sandy and Nan chuckle at our conversation and I smile at them.

"She says it like it's a bad thing."

"Sarah, there are moments in life you can't plan. Moments you'll miss because it's not part of your perfectly organized life."

"Prove it."

"I can't *prove* it."

"Exactly."

Kristen sits up straighter in her chair and levels her eyes on mine. "I can't prove it because you won't relax enough to *do* something spontaneous, to just get caught up in a moment."

"Easy on the melodrama," I quip, thankful no one else is in the salon.

"All I'm saying, Sarah, is that the best parts of life can't always be predicted. You can't constantly plan for every single experience."

"She's got a point," Sandy says, looking up from my feet. "Some of my best memories are of things that happened out of the blue. Things I never could have planned."

"Aha!" Kristen says, triumphant smile on her face. "Told you!"

I shake my head at Sandy. "And I pay you to do this to me?"

All three of the women laugh when I roll my eyes, but I can't help wondering if there might be a shred of truth in what they're telling me.

+ + +

"You have to help me." Kristen's lying on my bed, petting my other best friend, my three-year-old calico cat, Ringo. The bright pink on her freshly painted fingernails clashes against the red in his fur.

I put her soda on the dresser and open my own with a spoon I grabbed from the kitchen. I definitely don't want to mess up my fingernails after spending an hour and a half in that chair today.

"Help with what?" I take a sip, then put down my drink and grab Ringo from her grasp. I drop into the swing Mom had hung in my bedroom for my thirteenth birthday. It's not a playground swing. It's more of a front-porch kind of swing with a totally plush, hot-pink velvet cushion.

"Rock."

For a millisecond, I think I might pass out. My hand stills on Ringo's back, prompting him to move positions in an effort to get some more attention. The deep rumble of his purr vibrates against my knee.

Me? Help Kristen with Rock? *My* Rock?

"Geez, don't look so surprised. He was totally flirting with me at lunch."

Don't remind me.

"Since when do you need help with guys?" The fact that she's asking for my help is seriously comical. I've never even been on a date, unless you count the time my pimply cousin Nate took me to the eighth-grade dance. And I totally don't.

"I want him to take me seriously," she whines, her eyes wide and desperate.

I don't bother trying to stop myself from laughing out loud. "I think he takes you plenty serious."

"But he likes smart things. Like literature. I don't know anything about that kind of stuff. Nothing!" Panic brings her voice to a full screech and I hold up my hands to silence her.

"Be yourself, Kristen. If that's not good enough for him, then he doesn't deserve you." Okay, so there's a part of me that completely believes what I just said. But another, more evil part of me likes that Kristen has finally admitted she has a flaw.

"We're not living in some after-school special, Sarah. It isn't as simple as 'be yourself.'"

Ringo leans back and bites the hand I'm still resting on his back. "All right, already," I mumble to the cat as I resume stroking his tricolored fur.

"Yes! I knew you'd do it!" Kristen jumps off the bed and onto the swing, sending an angry Ringo to the floor with a yowl and a hiss.

I unwrap her arms from my neck. "No!"

"What?" she asks, arms crossed over her rounded chest. "But you said 'all right.' I heard you."

"I was talking to Ringo, Kris. I can't teach you about

literature in twenty-four hours or less. It's not like cramming for a test, for crying out loud. It's *literature*."

"And?" she asks.

"How many years do you think people have been writing?"

She shrugs, completely missing my point. "A lot?"

"Try thousands. How in the world am I supposed to teach you about literature that spans centuries? The stuff we've had in high school doesn't even scratch the surface. Don't you think he might notice you're not actually passionate about literature? It's more than just memorizing a bunch of names and dates. Why not introduce him to something you *are* passionate about?"

Kristen puts her hands in her lap, picking at the newly applied polish. "Like what?"

"Like taking care of animals. How many strays have you nursed back to health?"

"That's not serious enough, Sarah. Anyone can feed an animal."

I continue on, praying I can get through to her. "First of all, that's not true. You do more than feed them. Secondly, even if I gave you the CliffsNotes version of American literature, your knowledge base would be so full of holes he'd see right through it. I mean, unless you can figure out a way for me to talk *for* you . . . you're just going to have to do this on your own. And, trust me, I think your obvious assets will do the trick." They always do.

She raises her head, eyes sparkling with a mischief I haven't seen since we put shaving cream in Priscilla Hart's bra while she showered after a volleyball game. "What'd you just say?"

"That being yourself should be more than enough?" This is my mantra. And she was the one who first taught it to me.

"No! About you talking for me. That's the answer!" She bounces on the swing, threatening to bring the roof down on us.

I hop off the swing and stand in front of her. "Last time I checked, I wasn't a ventriloquist and you don't have a hole in your back for my hand."

"Not in person! We'd never pull that off."

Honestly. She's working my last nerve.

"Give up?" she asks.

"Will that shut you up?"

Kristen laughs, a maniacal sound that sends Ringo under the bed. If I thought I'd fit, I'd follow.

"It's so obvious," she says. "We'll talk online. Except you can write to him as me." Kristen's pointing at me and then herself, her ponytail bouncing up and down as she nods, reminding me of an excruciatingly perky flight attendant.

For the first time in my life, words fail me. I stare at her, pushing away the spark of resentment coming to life inside me. "You can't be serious."

"Totally," she whispers excitedly, her hands clapping under her chin.

"It'll never work. He's too smart to fall for something so lame." And I truly think writing to Rock as Kristen might kill me. Because he's absolutely perfect. *For me.*

When I take a breath to continue the list of reasons why we shouldn't do this, she drops the bomb. The one thing she knows will get me every time.

"I would do it for you." Her eyes turn teary and her voice is like a whisper. "You know I would."

And she has me. Because the honest-to-God truth is that she *would* do it for me. She'd do anything I asked. She always has.

Like the time I fell asleep with gum in my mouth and woke up with it matted in my hair. Mom hauled me to Penny's Pamper Palace to have it cut out and Kristen had her hair cut the exact same awful way. Or when we were in seventh grade and Mae Schroeder invited every single person in our class to her thirteenth birthday party except me, and Kristen jumped in with an impromptu party of her own, taking every last A-list kid with her. Mae spent her long-awaited birthday with a handful of geeks and wannabes while Kristen and I partied it up with everyone else.

I can't even visualize Rock in my head right now, because it's not about him anymore. It's about Kristen. My best friend. In my mind, there's not much of a choice.

If I have to choose between Kristen and a guy, or Kristen and myself, it'll be Kristen every time. I can't imagine doing anything to purposely hurt her.

I sit on the swing beside her and pull my legs up, resting my chin on my knees. "I'll think about it, but that's all I can promise."

✦ ✦ ✦

The moment I walk into journalism the following day, I regret my decision. Seriously. I'm totally counting on some tremendous karma payback for this kind of sacrifice.

Rock and Kristen are cozied up in our usual place and he's laughing at something she said. It's not until I drop my books on my desk that either one of them acknowledges me.

"Hey," Kristen says, keeping her eyes on Rock.

"What's so funny?" I regret the words the second they fly out of my mouth because I know how insecure I sound. Like some sort of wannabe clamoring to belong. Rock turns all of his attention to me, something I'm entirely uncomfortable with, especially when he takes the cursory pause when his eyes reach my nose. It takes everything inside me to not cover my face with something. A Boeing jet would do the trick.

When he finally pulls his eyes back to mine, he smiles. "I asked Kristen who her favorite poet was and she said Shel Silverstein."

"I was like totally kidding." Kristen shoots me a wide-eyed SOS look.

"Of course you were," I say. "Shel Silverstein's a great children's poet."

"I agree completely," Rock says, his eyes smiling. "I think 'One Inch Tall' is a remarkable piece of poetry, spotlighting the plight of the little people worldwide."

"Right." Kristen nods her head in serious agreement.

I force a laugh, giving a pointed look to Kristen. Does she honestly think he's being serious? Out of habit, I come to her rescue. "Hands down, Kristen's favorite poet is Maya Angelou."

I have obviously chosen her fake favorite well because she sits up in her seat, a surprised smile on her face. "I know who that is!"

Rock lowers his eyebrows and narrows his gaze at Kristen. "I hope so, since she's your favorite poet and all."

Realizing the absurdity of her comment, she flashes Rock one of her signature smiles. "What I meant was that . . . well, I've actually met her."

No, no, no, no, no . . . she did *not* just say that.

"You? Have met Maya Angelou? Quite possibly the greatest contemporary African American poet?"

Obviously, Kristen can't read the stunned look on my face, because she nods carelessly. Like she's actually telling the truth. If she can pull this off, she needs to head for Hollywood. Screw college.

"How'd you manage that?" Rock asks, obviously impressed. "I mean, from everything I've read about her, she's a pretty private person."

"How'd I meet her?" Kristen repeats. I know I should rescue her yet again, but I'm too curious to see how she digs her way out. Instead of looking directly at her, I busy myself by rummaging in my purse.

"Yeah, I mean, don't tell me you know Oprah, too," Rock chuckles.

"Actually, Sarah set it up." At the mention of my name in the middle of this train wreck, my hands stop moving and I glare at Kristen with a this-better-be-good look.

Kristen continues, focusing all of her attention on Rock. "Well, Sarah's mom's like really famous in Houston. She's a news anchor for channel six. You might have heard of her. Beth Burke?"

"Beth Burke's your *mom*?" Rock asks, and I'm so flattered

30

by his attention that I forget this is the only part of Kristen's story that's actually true.

"The one and only," I say.

Touching Rock's arm, Kristen pushes on. "She knows everyone. Her talent is completely wasted on the news. She totally belongs on *ET*." Kristen takes a deep breath before finishing her lie, which I guarantee she will later call a "tiny little fib." "Anyway, for my sixteenth birthday, she arranged for me to meet Maya Angelou when she was in town for some event." Kristen waves her hand in the air, like she can't be expected to remember such unnecessary details as *why* Maya Angelou was actually in Houston. Because, honestly, no one just drops into Houston for a little sightseeing. It's definitely the kind of place you visit because you have to.

"That's amazing," Rock says, his focus back on me. Honestly, if he has any brains at all, he'll know this is a total lie. It's just too unreal to be . . . real.

"Who's your favorite poet, Rock?" Kristen asks.

He pulls his eyes back to Kristen and leans in close. "Easy. Walt Whitman."

"Walt, huh?" Kristen asks, like she's actually heard his name before. "I'm sure Sarah's mom could arrange for you to meet him. Maybe by video or something."

Rock stares at Kristen for what seems like an eternity before bursting into a huge laugh. "You know what, Kristen? You're all right." He pats her hand, then squeezes it, and her chest turns a beautiful shade of brick red, a sure sign he's got her attention.

Kristen glances my direction before she says anything.

31

"You're okay, too, Rock. Tell you what, why don't you give me your e-mail and maybe we can chat."

Rock nods his head, a big smile still spread across his face. I can't believe it. He actually thinks she was kidding. While he scribbles his e-mail address on a sheet of notebook paper, I turn, shake my head at her, and put a finger in front of my mouth, trying to shut her up.

She totally ignores me and takes the paper he's given her, then folds it into a neat little rectangle and slides it into her purse.

The teacher's voice breaks through the ridiculous conversation. "Quiet down, class. It's time to get started."

When Rock faces the front of the classroom, Kristen looks at me with her hands held up in question.

"What?" she mouths silently.

I pull out my cell phone and text her. She glances at her vibrating cell and flips it open, and I watch the panic rise to her eyes as she reads it.

Walt Whitman died in 1892.

Everything has beauty, but not
everyone sees it.
—CONFUCIUS

Chapter Four

I shoot out of journalism, leaving Kristen to paw over Rock. There are some things I just don't need to see. Like the way Rock watches Kristen shimmy in and out of her desk or the way they look like they were made to be together. They seriously put Brad Pitt and Angelina Jolie to shame.

After making a detour to the restroom, I walk into lit class to find Rock leaning on Jacobi's desk, chatting it up like they're old friends. Rock stops his conversation midsentence when I walk past.

"Excuse me, Mr. Jacobi," he says.

"Of course," Jacobi replies with a grin. Like he knows something we don't.

I try my best to act like I don't know Rock's following me, like I don't feel the energy radiating off his body, like my palms always sweat when I walk into Jacobi's class.

Rock grabs my elbow before I can sit down. "You okay?" he asks.

My heart drops to the soles of my feet when I meet his eyes. His brows are lowered, dark eyes full of genuine concern. He leans in close, careful to keep our conversation private. But a quick glance around the room proves he's unsuccessful.

I force a plastic smile across my face. "Great!" I have to admit the tone in my voice is a little manic, kind of like what happens to Mom's voice when the teleprompter gets stuck on live television and she has to wing it. I pray my eyes don't look as crazed as hers, too.

"The way you darted out of journalism . . . ," he begins.

My eyes take a quick glance across the room of spectators, which happens to include Jacobi. I'm not averse to attention, especially when it doesn't center on my nose. But still, I don't need an audience right now.

I pull my hand from Rock's when I answer. "I just, um, I had to make a stop."

He nods, but the doubt in his eyes is easy to read. "If you're sure . . ."

"Pos-i-tive," I say, enunciating each syllable with entirely too much force and sounding like a complete and total social imbecile.

Jacobi closes the classroom door, finally breaking everyone's interest and prompting us to take our seats. Even when Jacobi begins talking, I can feel the heat of Rock's gaze on my back. No matter how hard I try, I can't focus on the lecture because my head is crammed with thoughts of how seriously my life sucks. I mean, it is totally unfair that I have finally met someone worth my time and instead of doing whatever I can to snag him for myself, I'm going to just hand him over to my best friend.

There absolutely has to be a way out of this. Think, Sarah. Think!

Rock taps my shoulder softly and I realize every pair of eyes in the room is staring at me. Oh. My. God. I've turned into that loser kid in class that never knows what's going on.

"Miss Burke?" Jacobi asks with an edge of irritation he typically reserves for the clueless. I've definitely seen him tear into plenty of loafers over the past couple years, but not me. Not even close.

Heat floods through me and I feel the tips of my ears burning. "I'm sorry, Mr. Jacobi. Can you repeat the question?"

Jacobi levels a look on me that would freeze water. "Rock, could you please repeat the question for Miss Burke?"

I don't dare turn around and face Rock, doing my best to act unaffected and failing miserably. Like I always get called out of a daydream.

"What's your definition of love?" Rock says, just loud enough for me to hear.

I nod to let him know I've heard him and take a deep breath before answering. I think about my love for Mom, for Kristen, for Ringo. What do the three things have in common?

"I guess my definition of love is caring about someone or something so deeply you can't imagine your life without them." There. That sounded pretty good, right?

Jacobi nods while pacing the front of the classroom. "Okay.

Let's take that one step further, Miss Burke. What are the characteristics of true love?"

Shrugging, I rack my brain for the right adjectives. "Selflessness."

"What else?"

Geez. He's totally not letting me off the hook. "Loyalty. Honesty."

"Anyone else want to add to that?" Jacobi asks, finally moving on with one last look that lets me know he'll be watching me. Like I'm one of "those" kids and not a straight-A student who could have easily graduated a year early.

I feel Rock leaning close to me and have to keep myself from shuddering when his warm breath tickles my neck. "Sure you're okay?"

Not trusting my voice, I shoot him a thumbs-up.

Rock stays where he is, breathing so close to my ear that if I turned, we'd be kissing. And, God help me, I want to kiss him so bad my lips are actually tingling.

I can feel his reluctance to believe my lie, but he finally settles back in his chair, leaving me cold and wishing like hell I wasn't such a loyal best friend.

✦   ✦   ✦

Rock follows me out of class, so close on my heels that we're practically dancing. When we make it to the hallway, he finally speaks.

"I know we just met, but I'm pretty good at judging people, and something's bothering you."

I continue snaking my way through the crowded hallway and Rock keeps right next to me, people clearing the way for him like the Red Sea parted for Moses.

"It's nothing," I mumble, wondering why I feel like a jerk for lying to him. I mean, he's almost a complete stranger, for crying out loud.

"I know you're not telling me the truth," he says as we reach my locker. "But I'll drop it."

I spin the lock and wrestle the old locker door open. Tossing my books inside, I step back so he can do the same. "Thank you."

"But if you need to talk about something, I'm a really good listener." His eyes are intense, as if the fate of the world rests on his ability to help me. He's freaking adorable.

"Okay," I say. "But, really, it's nothing. I'm just tired."

He slams the locker door closed, then pulls me into the flow of hallway traffic by my hand. Not to get all melodramatic, because that's definitely Kristen's department, but it's like our hands are a perfect match. There's nothing awkward about the firm grasp he has on me, and I like it. I really, really like it.

When we clear the mass of bodies rushing to make it to the cafeteria, Rock drops my hand, but not before Kristen sees Rock dragging me behind him. Her eyes are fixed on his hand, narrowed into deadly slits, until she realizes I'm the one with him. The familiar dimples crease her cheeks when she sees me.

"Hey," Rock says casually. "Been waiting long?"

Kristen shakes her head, turning her attention back to Rock. "Just got here. Y'all ready to eat?"

"Starved," Rock says, shooting Kristen a quick smile and a wink.

"Learn anything exciting in Jacobi's class today?" she asks, sliding back into sex-kitten mode. I have to force my eyes not to roll.

Rock shrugs with a grin. "We just talked a lot about love."

"Oh yeah? Like what?" Kristen asks, leading the way into the cafeteria.

"What defines love, which is really an interesting question, because it's different for everyone. I've never really thought about it before. Jacobi did his best to stump Sarah, but she had an awesome answer."

"Whatever," I say, blowing off the compliment.

"What'd you say?" Kristen asks, studying my face and trying to read my thoughts. She's always been way too good at that, and I'm hoping she can't read what I'm feeling about Rock. Because if she can, I'm going to need blasters and a force field to stay alive.

"I don't remember," I answer truthfully. The whole embarrassing event was a blur in my very crowded and confused mind.

"She said it was caring about someone so much you can't imagine life without them." Rock smiles at me and then looks back at Kristen. "Pretty good, huh?"

"Very," she says. "She's always had a way with words."

Rock looks back at me. "You also said it was selfless, honest, and loyal."

I'm so surprised he remembers what I said that I can't even muster a response. He was totally listening to me in class and I'm more than just a little flattered.

"Nice," Kristen says. "And what did you say, Rock?"

He shakes his head. "He didn't call on me, thank God. I'm not sure what I would have said. That's a tough question."

"Totally," Kristen agrees. "I'd hate to be in that class. Ugh."

"It's not all bad. Jacobi's pretty cool." Rock's defense of Jacobi makes me like him even more and I curse the rotten fate that put me in this situation. Rock grabs a sandwich plate and waits for me before following Kristen to the table.

When Kristen stops at a table in the back corner, Rock waits for us to sit. The guy's got some killer manners. My mom would definitely approve. I'm a little disappointed he's sitting next to Kristen until I remember I'm supposed to be helping her snag him—or at least thinking about it. It's enough to make me wish I had some excuse to leave the cafeteria.

"So, I was reading last night," Kristen begins, and my head shoots up, eyes wide. She's totally winging it and that never goes well for her. I do the only thing I know to save her from herself. I guess it's true what they say: old habits die hard.

"Did you pick up the new *Cosmo*?"

She stops cold and glares at me. "Very funny."

Rock looks at Kristen with obvious interest. "What were you reading?"

"Well, I have a list of books I want to read before I die and, trust me, that list is long. Really long."

I close my eyes, cringing inside. The only list Kristen's ever made was when she inventoried her shoe collection by designer. And a book list? *Please.*

"Impressive," Rock says, grinning.

What's impressive is Kristen's ease when she's lying about something so foreign to her. I mean, she might as well have made a list of the top ten economically impoverished countries in the world.

"So what book was it?" Rock asks again.

"*David Copperfield*," she says, a proud grin spread across her beautiful face.

"Charles Dickens at his best," Rock says appreciatively. I can tell by the look on his face he thinks he's hit pay dirt with Kristen. Beauty and brains don't often come together so seamlessly. If what she was saying were true, he'd be right. Honestly, Kristen is smarter than me in lots of ways. I don't know another human being who can mentally calculate the price of a clearance item that's been marked down eight times. But when it comes to academics, she's more of a do-what-it-takes-to-get-by kind of girl.

"It was the first book on my list. I mean, who doesn't love magic?" she asks proudly.

Oh no. No, no, no. I shake my head at her as discreetly as possible.

Rock stares at her, sandwich in hand. "Come again?"

I fix my eyes on Kristen, but she stubbornly ignores me by giving Rock her undivided attention. Fine, I think. Let her hang herself.

"Well, you have to agree that David Copperfield is one of

the most talented magicians in America. Right?" Kristen asks, eyes finally darting my direction. When she sees the look on my face, she realizes she's made a mammoth mistake.

Shaking his head, Rock laughs. "Girl, you're funny. Seriously funny."

She laughs nervously, looking at me with panicky eyes before turning her baby blues back on Rock. "Gotcha," she exclaims, and grabs his arm playfully.

Without hesitating, I jump in to save her. Talk about selfless love. "Kristen's always been interested in Charles Dickens and since *David Copperfield* is considered his most autobiographical novel, it makes sense she'd choose that book first."

"Exactly," Kristen says with a whoosh of relief. "What better way to get in old Charlie's head than to read *David Copperfield*?"

Rock smiles at me and then back at Kristen. "You're full of surprises, Kristen."

A wide, self-satisfied smile spreads across her face.

Like she didn't just nearly destroy her chances with Rock.

Like I hadn't just saved her from herself. Again.

Watching Rock eye Kristen like a starving man staring down a juicy steak is enough to make me lose my appetite.

This is going to be the longest year of my life.

+   +   +

"If I hadn't been there, you'd have been sunk," I say to Kristen from the passenger seat on the way home.

"I've already asked you to help me," she says with her signature sarcasm.

"I never said I would."

Kristen casts me a sideways glance, skepticism contorting her striking face. "Do you like him?" she asks.

"Who? R-Rock?" I stutter, keeping my eyes glued straight ahead and praying she doesn't notice the flush spreading up my neck. "No way. He's all yours."

"Are you sure?"

Am I sure? I almost laugh out loud, but sigh instead. "Positive."

"I mean, I can see how you'd like him." When she pauses, I shoot her a quick glance. She's biting her lip and tapping her thumbs on the steering wheel, lost in thought. "You have a lot in common."

"Nothing that matters," I say quickly. And it's true. What really matters is that Kristen and Rock are the kind of people that just go together. They make sense. Me and Rock? Complete nonsense.

"You'd tell me, right?"

I turn in my seat to face her. I would never betray her friendship, especially over a guy she's so consumed with. "You're being ridiculous."

With a semisatisfied sigh, she flops her head back, making me wonder how she can even see the road. "How was I supposed to know *David Copperfield* wasn't about the magician?" she whines.

"The fact that it was written in 1850 should have tipped you off," I say, grinning. Looking back at lunch, it was pretty funny. Only Kristen would think Charles Dickens could have written an entire novel about a twentieth-century magician in the nineteenth century. "Google things you don't know about before you talk about it. Or maybe you could just take my advice and talk about things that actually interest you. When did you decide that wasn't good enough? Every time you shoot your mouth off about things you know nothing about, you take the risk of digging yourself a hole you can't climb out of. I won't always be there to dig you out."

"I've been thinking about that," Kristen says.

I keep my face forward, afraid to look at her. She has a way of talking me into some really stupid schemes, and I already know this one is going to be the worst of the worst. "Nuh-uh," I say.

"Come on, Sarah. You promised you'd help me."

"I said I'd think about it," I correct her, concentrating on the houses zipping by. Anything but looking directly at her. It's like staring at the sun; one glance and you're a goner.

"What's to think about? It's me!"

I finally turn my unseeing gaze from the road and look at my best friend, the same girl who's stood by me year after year as I've been tormented by other kids. "Fine. I'll listen. But I'm not making any promises."

Kristen pulls into the driveway at my house and kills the engine.

"That's all I'm asking."

Though we travel the world over to find the beautiful,
we must carry it with us, or we will find it not.
—RALPH WALDO EMERSON

Chapter Five

"Okay, spill it," I say. I'm sitting on the bed cross-legged, with Ringo curled up tightly in my lap. I stroke his back, letting his rhythmic purring relax me like nothing else can.

"So, I've been thinking about how we can convince Rock that I'm smart."

"You *are* smart, Kris."

"Not like you are. Not like he is."

"Are you really sure you want to put this much effort into pretending you're something you're not? I mean, don't you think you'll get tired of lying to him? And what kind of foundation is that for a relationship, anyway?"

"Well, the way I see it, after I've proven how smart I am and he's totally fallen for me, then it won't be necessary to pretend anymore."

"You think he's going to just stop all conversation at some point?"

"We'll find other things to talk about. Things I actually know something about."

Hard as I try, I can't imagine Rock spending an afternoon watching Kristen try on twenty-three pairs of shoes. This is a guy who actually *thinks*. "You know, Kristen, you're a pretty good catch. I'm not convinced you need to do anything to get his attention. Seems to me you've already done that."

"I know," she says with her trademark smugness. "But I really think proving how smart I am is key."

"And how do you propose we do this?" I hope like hell she's got a killer new idea, because I'm drawing a complete blank. And I sure don't want to get into the whole imposter-conspiracy thing with her again.

Kristen pulls a folded scrap of paper out of her pocket and smiles. "Remember this?"

She tosses the paper to me and I unfold it. Inside is an e-mail address written in an unfamiliar handwriting. But I don't have to recognize the penmanship to know whose e-mail it is. The address says it all: rockcon@txmail.com.

"What are we going to do with Rock's e-mail address?" I ask, doing my best impersonation of the ever-clueless but well-meaning best friend. I mean, helping her learn more about lit is one thing, but lying . . . well, that's an entirely different issue altogether.

"Write him." Kristen whispers the idea I'd hoped she'd forgotten. I don't blame her for whispering; it's a plan doomed for utter disaster. And she doesn't even know it will leave me bloody and broken in the wreckage.

I'm shaking my head before she finishes the sentence. "When I said I'd *think* about helping you, I thought I'd be teaching you about things Rock's interested in. You know, actually *helping* you."

"What's the big deal? I'll tell you what I want to say and then you can write it in that way you have. Besides, you didn't say no. You said you'd think about it."

"Kristen, I just . . . I just can't do it," I say quietly, focusing on Ringo, who's rolled onto his back for some belly rubs. There are days I'd seriously trade my life for his. Starting with today.

"You have a way with words. Don't deny it, Sarah. How many times have you won first place for creative writing in the state competition? Four? Five?"

Seven, I think to myself. "That's different," I mumble.

"How is it different?" she asks, desperate for me to agree. I can read it in her face. She's counting on me and I hate to disappoint her. If I'm honest with myself, I like it when Kristen needs me, maybe because she needs me so rarely. It makes me realize my place in our friendship is as real and necessary as hers. Like we might actually benefit each other instead of me doing all the taking.

"First of all, it's deceitful. Second, it's a little creepy. I mean, I don't really want to get in the middle of your love life." Especially if it involves Rock.

"That's ridiculous. I'm not asking you to make it all up. Just help me. Come on," she pleads, taking my hands and squeezing them. "I'm begging you."

I chew on my bottom lip, scrambling for some excuse good enough to convince her I can't do this. But I come up empty.

46

And I'm supposed to have a way with words? How pathetic is it that I'm able to save Kristen from total self-destruction but not myself?

"Ground rules," I say, thoroughly disgusted with myself. I am so weak. I deserve to be miserable.

"Anything," she agrees.

"I decide when and how often. You can't expect me to drop everything and do this for you. I'm working to get a scholarship, remember?"

"Of course," she says, victory lighting her face. "Anything else?"

"You can't tell anyone—especially not Rock—that I did this. *Ever.*"

"Promise," she says, then reaches over for a suffocating hug. Kristen would normally hurt herself before letting an animal suffer, but she's so excited she completely ignores Ringo. He tears out of my lap, clawing my legs as he goes, but Kristen's oblivious to the damage she's causing my otherwise blemish-free legs.

Somehow I think that's a good indicator of where I'm headed . . . me suffering the battle wounds while Kristen rides the wave of triumph.

I've just agreed to help my best friend catch the guy of *my* dreams.

And people think I'm the smart one.

+ + +

By the time Mom gets home in the evening, I'm usually done with my homework and have started supper. Since it's just the

47

two of us, we stick to simple dishes with little or no cleanup: salads, sandwiches, takeout. Over the years, I've learned to be a pretty decent cook. I can follow a recipe like no other and have a basic understanding of how to cook different types of dishes. Our normal fare is low carb, low fat, and low taste; fish is a regular part of our health-conscious diet. Not exciting, I know, but it helps me keep my weight in check.

But after a day like this one, I need some serious comfort food so I can spend a night wallowing in the sad state of my personal life. I just need one night, then I'll be over it.

I think.

I put some skirt steak in the microwave for a quick defrost, then grab the flour, eggs, and milk. After pouring grease in the cast-iron skillet, I set the stove on high and focus on the batter for my favorite guilty pleasure: chicken-fried steak.

The next half hour involves me multitasking over the heaping meal I'm determined to prepare. Peeling potatoes, frying steak, and tossing together a to-die-for salad is oddly therapeutic.

When Mom glides through the door—and I do mean glide; she walks like she's riding on air—I'm washing dishes.

"Hmmm . . . ," she says, entering the kitchen with an appreciative smile. "I know what that smell means."

"No questions right now," I say, holding my hands up to squelch the interrogation I know she's about to launch. "Please. Let's just eat."

Mom and I know each other well; too well, sometimes. I guess I'm pretty transparent; it's not like I've ever intentionally kept something from her. Aside from the business about my nose, she's pretty cool. She can be a little obsessive about things she cares about, like work and me. But she's got a good heart and I know she loves me, which makes me luckier than a lot of kids I know.

Mom knows that chicken-fried steak is like my personal SOS. I guess the last time I made this meal was when I found out my ranking in our class had slipped from second to third. That was two years ago and I'm happy to say I've since solidly regained my status as second in our class. The guy in first place has an IQ as high as Mount Everest and a social life that makes mine downright enviable. I'm not willing to sacrifice that much for first place.

"Okay," she says, giving me a quick hug and kiss on the cheek. She kicks her high heels into the corner of the kitchen and grabs the plates and silverware.

"There's bread in the oven, if you want to get that out," I say, focusing on the task of transferring the potatoes to a serving dish. I know it seems silly to dirty another dish when we could just serve ourselves out of the pots, but Mom says it's uncivilized. She also thinks it's barbaric to eat any kind of sandwich without cutting it in half first.

We quietly go about the task of getting dinner on the table and then making our plates.

"Rough day?" Mom asks.

"Mom," I warn.

"Well, look at this feast, Sarah. It wouldn't take a genius to figure out something's bothering you."

Instead of answering, I chew my food, studying the remaining meat on my plate like it holds the secret to breaking the Da Vinci code.

"Sarah," Mom says quietly, barely above a whisper. "Talk to me."

I drop the fork on my plate and turn in my chair. "I'm just frustrated."

"About?"

Before answering, I try to decide if I should tell her the truth. She'd definitely take issue with me purposely deceiving someone, even if it was to help a friend. Mom is militant about honesty and justice.

"Guy stuff," I finally say. Not that I expect her to let it go at that.

"New guy?" she asks.

"How could it be an old guy?"

She smiles at me, like she knows what I'm feeling. And I guess in some ways she does. She did, after all, grow up with the same nose I have, so she was bound to go through the same teasing and insecurities. But it's hard to imagine her with any imperfection. I've only known her like she is today: impossibly flawless.

"What's the problem?" she asks.

"The usual," I reply, with maybe a little more bite than I intended. "There's this great guy who just moved here and we totally click. I mean, he actually likes school."

Mom raises her eyebrows. "How's this a problem?"

"He's made it clear he's interested in someone else."

Mom tilts her head like a puppy who's just heard a new sound. "Who?"

"Kristen," I say in full pout. I'm not proud of it, but it's my right to throw a tiny little fit. It's so unfair.

"Oh, well, that definitely muddies the water, doesn't it?"

Muddies the water? Who talks like that?

"A little," I say sarcastically. "Not only that, she wants me to help her win him."

"How are you supposed to do that?"

It's a good question I can't answer honestly. "Just help her understand more about . . . everything. Things he's interested in. Things she knows nothing about."

Mom laughs, then takes a drink of water before being able to talk. "Kristen is concerned she isn't good enough? For a guy? Since when?"

"Since Rock," I say, enjoying Mom's response just a little bit. It's good to know I'm not the only one who recognizes the absurdity of the situation.

"Rock?" she asks, eyes wide, eyebrows sky high. "That's his name?"

I nod, grinning. "His name is actually Rockford, but he goes by Rock. Rock Conway."

"Well, that's quite a name. Does he have some brains to go with that?"

"Afraid so," I tell her. And I really mean it. It'd be so much easier to act like he didn't matter if he had the IQ of a tick. "He's pretty bright."

"So what are you going to do about this guy?" she

asks. I hate it when she slips into investigative-journalist mode.

"Nothing."

"That hardly seems like the right decision if you really like him. Maybe you should talk to Kristen about it. Why don't you spend a day at the mall like you used to and tell her how you feel?"

I think about how Kristen reacted to Rock holding my hand and the way she questioned me about liking him on the way home. "The mall part sounds good. The talking-about-Rock part? Don't think that'd be smart."

Mom moves the food around on her plate, thinking. "You know, it's getting harder to help you with your problems. It was a lot easier when your biggest dilemma was who to invite to a slumber party." She grabs my hand and gives it a quick squeeze. "Why don't you come to the station tomorrow after school? We've got a new reporter I want you to meet. She's fresh out of college; you'll love her."

Without waiting for my answer, she pushes her barely touched plate away from herself as she stands. She doesn't have to say what she's thinking; I've heard her say it a thousand times. *The camera is unforgiving.*

I smile and nod. "I'll get the dishes. Why don't you change out of your work clothes?"

"What'd I ever do to deserve you?" she asks as she walks out of the kitchen.

Our house normally has plenty of silence since it's just the two of us. Mom married her high school sweetheart right after she graduated, and then promptly divorced him six months later. She never married again; she said she just didn't have the time. It's hard to date when you work eighty hours a week.

Husband or not, she wanted children. So she did what any self-respecting, liberated, twentieth-century woman would do: she was artificially inseminated. And voilà, here I am.

Officially, my father is known as number 55341. What I know about him is that he was in medical school and was tall and athletic. What I got from him I'll never really know since I have a distinct aversion to blood, stand only five feet five, and have seen crippled dogs run better than me. I don't wonder who he is; I don't pass people on the street and think "That might be my dad." I don't daydream about missed father-daughter moments and I don't cry during Hallmark commercials.

I am decidedly like my mother, which is something I embrace. There are worse people to emulate than a successful news anchor in a market the size of Houston.

Still, I wouldn't mind having a guy show some interest in me.

But looking at my reflection in the window over the sink, I'm reminded of the reason my social life has been lackluster. And for the hundredth time since meeting Rock, I wonder if Mom's right.

Maybe it's time to fix the one thing holding me back.

My nose.

There is no excellent beauty that hath not some
strangeness in the proportion.
—SIR FRANCIS BACON

Chapter Six

After school the next day, I drive into the parking lot outside the food-court entrance at the mall, looking for the closest space while Kristen rambles endlessly about the stores she intends to hit while we're here. By the time we step through the automatic doors and inhale the mixed aroma of Cinnabon and french fries, I'm mentally exhausted. Shopping with Kristen is not for the weak.

"I want something kind of dressy for Friday," she says, walking so quickly I have to double-step to keep up. "Don't you think?"

"If that's what you want." I know a rhetorical question when I hear one. "It's just Amber's usual back-to-school thing. Don't know that you really need to dress up."

Kristen stops and turns to face me. "It's the *only* back-to-school party, Sarah. It sets the social tone for the rest of the year."

I put a hand over my mouth to keep from laughing. "Wow. Sounds serious."

"Not funny." She pouts, then grabs my wrist and pulls me into the Buckle. "You may be content to commit social suicide but I'm not going to let you. I swear, if I didn't know any better, I'd think you were a loner."

Kristen's probably right. If it weren't for her, I'd spend most nights at home studying or working on college applications. She's mastered the art of dragging me out of the house and I'm always glad when she does.

One of the things I love most about Kristen is her financial prowess. She's going to make some man very happy one day. She may love to shop but she's as frugal as they come.

"Here," she orders, "take these and try them on while I look for me. The most expensive item in there is $14.99. Even I can afford that."

"Excuse me?"

Kristen stops raking through the sale rack and looks up fully exasperated. "Just try them on."

"What if I don't want to go to the party Friday?" Sometimes teasing her is just too easy.

"You're killing me, you know that?" She points to the dressing room. "Get shaking, Sarah. And I want to see every single thing on you."

With the clothes draped over my arm, I walk into the dressing room with a smile on my face.

By the time we walk out of the Buckle, I've bought a red scooped-neck shirt that will look perfect with my favorite jeans and flip-flops. Kristen managed to unearth an eighty-dollar dress that was on sale for twelve. She always surprises me with what she can find in the deepest, darkest recesses of any store.

We grab a couple of Diet Cokes and a large order of fries to split.

Kristen sits across from me at a food-court table securely fastened to the floor with screws the size of railroad ties. Do they really think someone is going to steal this junky stuff?

She grabs a handful of fries and dips them in the ketchup. "Think I should ask Rock to the party on Friday?"

My heart slams to a stop. "Rock?"

She smiles deviously. "Yeah, Rock. You *do* remember him, right? He's the tall, handsome guy we—"

I hold up my hands to stop her description. "Of course I remember him. But you barely know him. Don't you think it might be too soon?"

"Yet," she says. "But I intend to fix that."

"I thought we were going together." As much as I wanted to see Rock again, I wasn't sure I was ready to face a party without Kristen by my side. We've always done those things together.

"That's the beauty of inviting him to the party. The three of us can go together. It won't be like a 'date'—it'll just be a group of friends going out together. I won't leave you stranded. Promise."

"It's not that," I say, desperate to find the right words to change her mind. Going with Kristen and Rock sounds worse than going alone. "What if he's not the partying kind of guy?"

"With a face like that? Trust me, he's the partying kind. Maybe not a beer-guzzling, football-playing kind of partyer, but he has definitely seen a party or two."

Mom's advice comes back to me and I know that if I'm going to say something about my feelings for Rock, this is the time to do it.

"About Rock . . ." I drum my fingernails on the side of my cup, my eyes glued to my straw like it holds the winning lottery numbers. I force myself to look at her. If I'm going to do this, I'm going to do it right.

Kristen nods, but her eyes are like laser beams directed at two junior high kids who are walking by slowly. One of the boys is laughing hysterically and the other has his arm bent at the elbow and stuck out in front of his face like it's a bird beak.

I give Kristen a wink, take a quick swallow of my soda, then walk to the boys. I hook my arms around theirs like they're my prom dates. I lower my head and whisper softly so only they can hear.

"When I saw the two of you walk into the food court wearing jeans six sizes too big, I didn't stand up and make a scene, did I?"

Both boys shake their heads quickly.

"I could have pulled my pants way down past my butt, letting the whole world see the pink lace panties I chose to wear today. But I didn't. And do you know why I didn't?"

More nervous glances pass between the boys. "No," the one on my right mumbles.

"Because I have a little something called decency. Respect.

The three of us have something in common. All three of us make pretty easy targets for bullies. But there is one significant difference. Want to know what that is?"

Their silence makes me grin. I'm taking way too much pleasure out of making them squirm.

"The difference is that you can change the way you look with a cruise through the mall. A quick trip through Old Navy, and you can have a closet full of jeans that actually fit. Me? I was born with this nose. So I take offense to your ridicule."

The boys blush, eyes still on the ground, feet shuffling restlessly.

"Now . . . where's my apology?"

"Sorry," they grumble in unison.

"Alrighty, then. You two have yourselves a fabulous day." I pat their shoulders with two quick, forceful taps and watch them slink off in shame. I walk back to the table, where Kristen is smiling. She loves it when I stand up for myself almost as much as I do.

+ + +

When Kristen and I arrive at school the next morning, Rock is getting out of his truck and walking toward us. He looks amazing in a dark blue Hurley T-shirt and well-worn jeans. His hair is still damp; my fingers itch to run through it. A flash of him in the shower shoots through my brain. Just the thought of his muscles fully bared is enough to render me speechless.

"Damn, he's hot," Kristen utters as she slams her car into park.

I can only manage a nod and step out of the car with my backpack and purse slung over my shoulder.

"Morning, girls," he calls out, waiting for us in the middle of the parking lot.

Kristen waves and walks with a purpose I've never seen before. She half slithers, half skips to where he stands, never looking back to make sure I'm following. When Kristen reaches him, she starts walking toward the school, but Rock waits for me. As soon as she realizes she's alone, she quickly returns to his side, shooting me an irritated look as if I'm purposely holding them up.

Rock smiles wide, nearly stopping me in my tracks. "We're twins," he says.

I look down and realize he's right. Like Rock, I'm wearing a dark blue shirt and jeans. "So we are," I say as unaffectedly as possible. Once Kristen realizes the wardrobe coincidence, she'll spend the rest of the day obsessing over why she isn't wearing something similar.

"Except you look about a million times better than I do," he says warmly.

Geez, would he quit being so freaking perfect?

"Hey, either of you know Amber Wakely?" he asks.

Kristen stops walking. "Of course we do. Why?"

Rock shrugs his muscular shoulders. "She asked me to a party on Friday night. Sounded fun."

"Funny you should ask about that," Kristen says. "We just went shopping for that party last night."

"How would you feel about our riding together? I want to

go but don't love the thought of walking in and not knowing a single person there."

I stand outside the conversation, feeling fully forgotten.

"Sounds great," Kristen breathes. "Why don't you pick me and Sarah up at my house?"

"That'll work," he says, tossing me a quick smile.

I fumble around in my head for something witty to say, but all I can come up with is, "I'm going to run ahead. I need to talk to Mrs. Freel before class starts. See you in there." Of course today, of all days, we have first period together because of a schedule change for the DARE assembly. I won't be able to escape them for long.

Before either one of them can protest, I take off in a half jog and I know how ridiculous I look. But I'd rather run like a clumsy, newborn moose than listen to Kristen ooze her charm all over Rock. And worse, watch him suck it all up.

I'm the first one in Mrs. Freel's class. I don't have a single reason to talk to her, but I'm sure not going to get caught in a lie, so I take my seat and open *The Scarlet Letter*. The novel was part of my summer reading list before my junior year, so I've read it before. But Jacobi is famous for pop quizzes, so I'd better be prepared.

The class begins filling up and there's still no sign of Ken and Barbie. At 7:59, the two of them race in just as Mrs. Freel is closing the door.

"Cutting it a little close, aren't you?" she sneers. Nothing irritates her more than tardiness, something she and I have in common.

"Yes, ma'am," Rock answers. "Won't happen again."

The entire class watches them walk back to our corner of the room, me included. I mean, let's face it. It's hard not to stare.

Before Rock takes his seat, he turns the full wattage of his killer smile on me. "Get your business taken care of?" he whispers.

I nod, incapable of muttering anything intelligible.

He crams his too-tall body into the old desk and leans back with a sigh.

I do my best to focus on Freel's lecture about elements of a headline news story (like I don't already know—I could practically teach this class), but for the life of me, I can't focus on anything but the tiny little leaf wedged into Rock's still-damp hair.

When Kristen reaches up to grab the leaf from his hair, she turns to me with a victorious smile.

The bagel I'd slammed for breakfast lands with a solid thud in the bottom of my stomach. Looks like they found something to do besides talk after all.

✦   ✦   ✦

"Omigod, Sarah. It was amazing." Kristen drops into the seat across from me in the library during our study hall.

"I'm sure it was," I say, wishing I could escape the blow-by-blow she's about to deliver. I don't bother looking up from *The Scarlet Letter*, not really reading but desperate to block her out.

"He started teasing me about being so small, and I told him I could totally take him." Kristen continues rambling while I stare at the book in front of me, willing myself to read the words on the page instead of listening to her recount every millisecond of their morning tryst.

"Then he tripped me and we wound up on the lawn."

"Wow," I mumble, dying a little with each word.

"Geez, could you show a little excitement?" she complains. "I mean, this is what we're trying to accomplish, remember?"

How could she know that, for me, watching them together is the equivalent of watching someone torture a defenseless animal? I had my chance to tell her how I feel and blew it.

"So anyway, I've written the first letter," she says with an exasperated roll of her eyes, unzipping her binder in one smooth motion. I can't help but notice she's already managed to destroy the organization I'd put in place for her. It's taken her less than a week to obliterate my efforts.

"Honestly, Kristen." Taking her binder, I make quick work of filing the papers back in their rightful spots before sliding it back across the desk to her. "What's it take?"

She ignores me as she grabs a sheet of paper from the back of her binder. "I know where everything is. That's all that matters."

When she moves the paper in front of me, the first thing I notice is a lot of scribbling and drawing. Hearts, flowers, that kind of preteen thing. Nestled in the middle of the artwork is a tiny paragraph in Kristen's familiar bubbly handwriting. Most people outgrow their junior high cursive script, but not Kristen. She's still putting hearts above her *i*'s and ending all dangling letters like *g* and *j* in curlicues. A hopeless romantic.

I read the words scrawled on the paper. It doesn't take long.

Rock,
I am so glad you have come to Houston.
I hope we get to know each other better.
Much better.
Call me . . . 555-0250
Love, Kristen

I look up from the note.

"I know it's awful. Can you fix it? Make it . . . I don't know . . . unforgettable?" She looks at me, hope shining in her eyes.

Can I? Sure.

Should I? No.

Will I? Probably.

"Before I even attempt to rewrite this, you need to have a clear purpose. Are you writing to prove you're intelligent? You *are*, you know." I push the letter closer to her.

Kristen rolls her eyes again. "Not about the right things. That's why I need you."

"Well, it's not exactly like you can send a letter with a list of the things you know, Kristen. You have to slip it into conversation."

She looks at me like I've told her she has to solve a quadratic equation in the next ten seconds. "I have no idea how to do that."

"Okay, let's start with this. Let's focus on the feelings you have for him and forget about proving something to him. What did you think the first time you saw him?" I ask.

"He's smoking hot."

I chuckle at her honesty and remember thinking the exact same thing. "Okay, so honest is good, but maybe it's too much. Did your stomach flip? Did you begin to sweat? What kind of reaction did you have to him?"

Kristen squints her eyes, thinking back to that morning. "My heart was definitely racing, but I didn't sweat. Gross."

Yet my hands sweat every time I lay eyes on him. She'd definitely have something to say about that.

"That's a start," I say. "You could say something like 'When I see you, my heart dances.'"

"Isn't that kind of corny?" she says, frowning.

"Yeah," I agree. "How about 'You set my heart on fire'?"

"Ooh! That's good! Write that down." Kristen taps the paper lying on the table between us.

I grab a pencil from her open binder and scrawl the phrase on the back of her letter. "What kinds of things do you want to do with Rock?"

She arches an eyebrow. "Do I really have to spell it out?"

"Okay, you little hussy, keep it clean. What would be your dream date? Maybe you should ask him out."

"Me? Ask a guy out? I don't think so," she snorts.

"You're already going to be with him on Friday night. What's the big deal? Do you want to go out with him or not?" I ask, frustrated at her stubbornness. If I thought Rock would say yes and it wouldn't obliterate my friendship with Kristen, I'd have asked him out the first day we met.

"Well, yeah, but . . ."

"No buts. This is your chance to show him you're a risk

taker. That you're not afraid to go after what you want, especially him."

"There's always the movies," she offers with a shrug.

"That's your dream date? Come on, you can do better than that." I shake my head and do the thinking for her. There has to be *something* unique they can do. Something Rock probably hasn't done or seen before.

"I've got it," I tell her. "How about the Aquarium? You could go there for dinner. I doubt he's been there before and even if he has, it's still a great date restaurant."

"I love that place. Definitely." She taps the paper again. "That should do it. Let's go send it."

"Now?" I ask, head spinning. Surely she doesn't think I'm going to be able to just whip this out in thirty seconds.

"Yes, now. When else?" She stands and walks to the bank of computers lining the perimeter of the library. "Come on."

Fighting every shred of common sense inside me, I stuff the novel into my binder and follow her to the computer, where she's already busy logging on. I stand behind her, letter in hand.

She opens her e-mail account, clicks Compose, types in Rock's e-mail address—which she's already memorized—and stands. "It's all yours."

Of course it is, I think as I take a quick glance at the clock, then drop into the seat. "We've only got eight minutes."

"That's more than enough time for a supersmart genius like you. Get busy." She rubs my shoulders like she's prepping a boxer for the next round.

I shake her off. "Back up a little. Geez."

She plops into the seat next to me as I put my hands on the keyboard, staring at the flashing cursor. It's totally mocking me.

Tapping my fingers on the keys, I look at my notes, then begin typing. After a couple of false starts, I finally get in the groove and the words flow. Kind of.

I know this may seem a little forward, but I have to tell you that every time I see you, your smile sets my heart on fire. I can't explain it, but I've never felt this way before. Join me for dinner at the Aquarium Saturday night. My treat.
Love, Kristen
555-0250

"It's too short," I say.

"No, it's just right." Kristen's smile is glowing and it's hard not to let her joy rub off on me just a little. For a second, I can even pretend my every waking moment isn't filled with thoughts of the very guy she's—we're—writing.

"Maybe we should add something specific about his smile," I say, more to myself than anyone.

"Like how precious his crooked teeth are?" she says quickly. "It's so adorable."

"I'm not sure. It's just missing something." I continue tapping the keys. "What about . . ." I click the cursor before the last sentence and add a new one, then reread the new message.

I know this may seem a little forward, but I have to tell you
that every time I see you, your smile sets my heart on fire.
I can't explain it, but I've never felt this way before. There's
something in your smile that makes me feel alive. Join me for
dinner at the Aquarium Saturday night. My treat.
Love, Kristen
555-0250

I swivel the screen so Kristen can see it, feeling pretty
damn proud of my ability to take her grade-school letter and
turn it into something spectacular in three minutes flat.

Kristen reaches over and hugs me. "You're amazing.
Send it!"

"Are you sure?" I ask. "There's no turning back after this."

"Positive." She reaches around me, commandeers the mouse,
then clicks Send.

Somebody shoot me.

It is amazing how complete is the delusion
that beauty is goodness.
—LEO TOLSTOY

Chapter Seven

I make it to the station just minutes before Mom goes live for the five o'clock broadcast, looking forward to dinner and not so forward to meeting another rising news star.

"You're finally here," she says, eyes closed in the makeup chair as Marta continues her work on Mom's eyelids. Don't ask me how she knows I'm here; mother's intuition or something. "I was getting worried."

"Sorry," I say. "Hi, Marta."

"How's life treating you, Sarah?" she asks, never taking her eyes off Mom. Marta's been Mom's stylist and makeup artist for years. Her twin sons just turned thirteen, so she always looks a little frazzled and vaguely irritated.

"Pretty good," I answer. "How are the boys?"

Marta looks up from Mom's face and I can see the dark circles under her eyes. "Making me wonder why I ever went through all those years of infertility treatments to create them."

I laugh, knowing Marta loves the boys more than anything. "That bad, huh?"

"Just typical teenage-boy stuff." She dusts Mom's face with an oversized powder brush, then leans back to study her handiwork. "You're done, Beth."

Mom opens her eyes and studies her face in the mirror as she takes off the protective drape snapped behind her neck. "Great job as always, Marta. Thanks."

Mom stands and grabs my hand. "I'm on in four minutes, so we'll have to talk later."

"Bye, Marta," I call out as Mom drags me from the room.

"Later, gorgeous!" Marta answers, already cleaning the workspace she insists on keeping immaculate. It's just one of the many reasons I adore her.

Mom turns her full attention to me and I'm struck by her stunning face. Does she realize how beautiful she is or does she still see the insecure girl with the gargantuan nose when she looks in the mirror? "You look great, Mom."

A warm smile brightens her face. "Thanks, sweetie. You look pretty marvelous yourself."

I look down at the blue jeans and T-shirt I've worn all day. "Right."

"Where do you want to watch? From the stage or the sound room?"

"Definitely the stage," I say. I'm not in the mood for a bunch of chitchat with Mom's producer, Vic, who's been gunning to date her since the first day she arrived over ten years ago. He's a nice-enough guy but I get the feeling he's trying to play dad to me. Not cool.

"Okay," she says. "Don't leave. I still want you to meet Jen and then we have a dinner date, remember?"

"I'll be right here," I say, pointing to my usual seat at the edge of the room that gives me a great view of the news desk.

Mom takes her seat at the right of her coanchor, David Newlund. He's a pretty decent guy, even if he's totally self-absorbed. One of the things I've learned about this business is that most on-air journalists, especially anchors, have a tendency to be full of themselves. Even Mom can get that way from time to time, which is one of the reasons I'm sticking to print, where the news is all about the facts. Nothing else matters. Not the way you dress, the way you look, or how old you are.

Watching the two of them behind the glass desk, it's easy to see how anchors become that way. They're spectacular forty-somethings with perfect hair, perfect teeth, and perfect clothes. The two of them together make a showstopping anchor team; they've been ranked first in the Houston market since they paired up nearly six years ago.

When the director calls out the one-minute warning, Mom takes one last look at the papers in front of her. I know from years of following her around the station that she and David have spent the better part of the day going over the news stories with Vic, deciding which stories to report and in which order. The fact that she and David keep the papers in front of them during the newscast has never made sense to me. They keep their eyes on the teleprompter, only ad-libbing when they have to stretch for time.

I watch the newscast, mesmerized by the range of emotions

that play over Mom's face, alternating between amused and deadly serious as the news story she's reporting warrants. Anyone who thinks reporters aren't actors is fooling themselves. I know that Mom's genuinely upset when she reports a murder or fatal car wreck, but to seamlessly transition from that story to a feel-good story about a dancing pig . . . well, that takes talent. And Mom's got it in spades.

Over the years, Mom's not so gently pushed me to follow in her footsteps. And there's a huge part of me that wants to do just that. I've grown up at this station, watching news stories unfold before my eyes. It's an addictive industry, really. Especially if you thrive in an environment where no two days are the same. But I have my reasons for insisting on print journalism.

Coming to the station is always tricky for me because they have a huge turnover, especially with all the interns they hire. So a cruise through the station is uncomfortable as people try not to stare at the anchor's daughter's enormous nose. And I'll give them credit; they always try to look me in the eyes, but it never quite works. Without even realizing it, their eyes wander back to the gigantic beak I've been graced with.

Mom says I'm stubborn to a fault, but that's really not it. I'm not refusing to get a nose job just to assert my independence. It's more an issue of being determined to accept who I am. Mom devoted an enormous amount of energy into raising a self-assured young woman, and now that I've become that, she's irritated I won't cave to society's idea of beauty.

Not that I don't consider the wretched rhinoplasty every

now and then. I'm only human. But I've spent so many years insisting I can live with my nose that I actually kind of believe it.

When the news finally wraps, Mom says a few quick good-byes to the cameramen before coming to get me.

"Great, as always," I say with a smile, proud of Mom and all she's accomplished.

"Like you ever watch," she says, which is basically true. I only watch her in person. Somehow, seeing her on television isn't the same for me. She just never seems real.

I follow her down the wide corridor that leads to the enormous newsroom, affectionately referred to as "the pit," divided only by cubicle half-walls and a menagerie of filing cabinets and desks. This is truly the heart of the newsroom and I defy anyone to walk through this space and not get a little rush of adrenaline. I wave and smile at the faces I know as we move to Mom's office, one of the few enclosed rooms along the back wall.

Once inside, she quickly removes her jacket and hangs it on a hook behind her door. She grabs the clothes hanging in her armoire. "Let me change and then we'll find Jen before going to dinner."

Mom slips into her private bathroom as I sit in the buttery-soft leather chair behind her desk, which is littered with Post-its, notepads, and about two dozen different pens and pencils. I have to stop myself from organizing the mess. The last time I did that, she nearly had a heart attack.

She emerges from the bathroom looking like a model for

Ann Taylor, wearing crisp white capris with a pale yellow cardigan set, which is stunning against her spray-tanned skin and shoulder-length blond hair. "Let's find Jen," she says.

Mom has a history of introducing me to up-and-coming reporters at the station in the hopes that their excitement and newfound success will light a fire in me. I gave up fighting these meetings years ago.

I follow Mom as she walks through the newsroom, keeping my head down when she peeks over cubicle walls. Don't want to frighten the newbies by throwing my nose into their already-crowded cubicles.

"There she is," she says, waving at a tall, beautiful brunette leaning over a printer and looking like she might tear it apart and throw it out the fourth-story window behind her.

"What's the problem, Jen?" Mom asks, like she would have a clue about how to help her. She knows just enough about technology to send and receive e-mails. Even that's a chore for her.

Jen lets out a frustrated sigh. "Bum equipment." She drops the screwdriver onto the table and extends her hand. "You must be Sarah. I've heard so many wonderful things about you."

I take her hand, noticing her firm handshake, something Mom insists every professional woman must master. "It's nice to meet you, Jen."

"Jen Masters," she says, filling in the last name for me. I'm stunned at her ability to look me in the eyes, not wavering for even a second. Impressive.

"How long have you been working at the station?" I ask, easily slipping into my own form of investigative journalism. I have a bank of questions for these kinds of meetings.

"Just under a month," she says, her velvety voice warm. I like her instantly, unlike so many others I've met before her. Despite her drop-dead-gorgeous looks, she's surprisingly real.

"Where did you work before you came here?" I ask.

She laughs with a small roll of her eyes. "I was a reporter in Texarkana."

Anyone with a morsel of knowledge about broadcast journalism knows that a move from Texarkana to Houston is the equivalent of jumping from T-ball to the World Series.

"Congratulations," I say.

"Thanks, Sarah. I'm really excited to be here." She casts a disparaging glance at the ancient printer on her desk. "Well, I *would* be if I could get this piece of junk working."

"Here," I say, moving around her desk to the printer. "Let me look."

"Oh, no. That's okay. You two go on to dinner."

Mom waves her comment away. "Let her try. She's a genius with this kind of thing."

I open the printer door and pull out the toner, then pull about a dozen torn pieces of paper from the machine. When I replace the toner cartridge and reset the printer, papers begin printing and Jen sighs in relief. "I owe you."

"No problem," I answer. "Simple fix."

Mom laughs. "Everything's simple for Sarah."

I have to stop myself from laughing out loud. There are a few things in my life that I don't find simple. Not the least of which is my personal life.

"Are you joining us for dinner?" I ask Jen, hoping she is. There's something about her that I like, something that tells me she's worth knowing.

"Sorry," she answers. "I've got a deadline to meet. And thanks to this printer, I'm already running behind. Maybe next time."

"Count on it," Mom says, then turns to me. "Ready to go, sweetie?"

"Definitely." I turn to smile at Jen before following Mom. "It was really nice to meet you, Jen."

And for the very first time since I began meeting Mom's coworkers over a decade ago, I honestly mean it.

✦ ✦ ✦

Kristen practically pounces on me when I jump into her Jeep the following morning. "What happened to you last night?" she demands.

"What do you mean?" I ask, doing my best to keep up with her rapid-fire words.

"What do I mean?" she repeats, eyes wide, voice high and screechy. "What I mean is where were you when I called?"

"I was at dinner with Mom. What's the emergency?"

"Rock, that's what!"

Okay, now she's got my attention. "Rock?"

"Yes. Rock."

"What about him?" I ask, heart pounding in my chest like the bass drum on the high school drum line.

"He *replied*."

"Replied to what?" I ask, lost for the sweetest little second before reality slaps me in the face. "Wait. He *replied*? What'd it say?"

Instead of answering, she pulls a folded sheet of paper from the glove box and drops it on my lap. I stare at it, dread filling my empty stomach.

"Open it!" Kristen demands, clapping her hands in urgency.

I do as she says, unfolding the paper like a rattlesnake might jump out at me, and read the printed e-mail.

Kristen,
Thanks for the e-mail. I'd love to go to the Aquarium. But I insist on paying. That's a deal breaker.
"Barkis is willin'."
Rock

Barkis is willin'.

It's like a punch in the gut just reading it. Knowing he wrote it about Kristen makes me positively nauseous.

"Did you e-mail him back?" I ask, praying she hasn't but almost wishing she has. I know that makes me a crummy friend and I hate I even thought it. Why would I want her to embarrass herself like that? Mom was right: men can ruin a woman's other relationships.

Kristen pulls away from the curb, then makes a sound

somewhere between a howl and a laugh. "Not hardly. I don't even understand what that quote means. How I am supposed to respond to that? And what am I going to do at dinner? I mean, if he starts talking like that, I'm going to fall flat on my face."

I clap my hand over her mouth to squelch her rising hysteria. "Calm down." Removing my hand, I look at her. "Take three deep breaths."

I take the breaths with her, trying to think through her legitimate concerns. "Okay, are you ready to talk about this?" Am *I*?

She nods, eyes on the road, white knuckles grasping the steering wheel in a death grip.

"First of all," I say, "you have *got* to relax. I've never seen you this uptight before."

"I've never felt so stupid before. I'm totally freaking out. Who the hell is Barkis? And what, exactly, is he willing to do?"

I can't stop myself from smiling. "The quote is really pretty clever. Barkis is a character from *David Copperfield*. He sent the message 'Barkis is willing' to the woman he was in love with, but she wasn't interested. His persistence paid off; he finally won her over in the end."

Kristen slaps her hand over her chest, mouth agape. "Oh. My. God. That's so sweet!"

And just like that, he's stolen my heart and broken it. There's finally a guy out there that has a clue and he's got his eyes set on Kristen, a girl unlikely to appreciate his intelligence.

It was as if he'd written to me, not Kristen. Me. Like we had our own secret literary code that only he and I would understand.

"Let's talk about dinner," I say. "He said yes and he wants to pay. Those are good things. That means he's got some maturity and sense about him. It's supersweet that he wants to treat you to dinner."

"What about the quote? What if he talks like that?"

I fold the e-mail back up and return it to the glove box. "First of all, he's just feeding off what you told him you were reading. And second, no one actually talks like that. If he tries to start a conversation about *David Copperfield*—or some other novel you've never read before—then change the subject to something you're more comfortable with."

Kristen chews on her lip, her breathing back to normal. "I can do that, right?"

"Totally." Maybe.

"You have to help me get ready. Promise you will," she pleads, regressing to toddler tactics. I swear, if she wasn't driving she'd be on her knees, pulling on my shirt as she begs.

"The last thing you need is me telling you what to wear. That's like Tyra Banks getting clothing advice from Lady Gaga."

Of course, that's not entirely true. I definitely have a style . . . but it's my own and about a million miles away from Kristen's. The thought of watching her get ready for her first official date with Rock is enough to make me nauseous.

She slams her hand on the steering wheel. "You *have* to, Sarah!"

"I don't know, Kris, it just seems like overkill. When did you become so utterly incapable of being yourself?"

She totally ignores the question, which, I suppose, is rhetorical. We both know the answer, after all. "I'm not taking no for an answer. Unless you've got a date of your own, you *will* be there to help me get ready."

I shake my head, wishing I actually had a date. Maybe then she'd get off my back. Maybe then watching her with Rock wouldn't hurt so much.

I stare at her but stay silent.

"Promise me," she says, tears welling in her eyes right on cue. She seriously belongs on the big screen. "I can't do this without you."

"Fine," I grumble.

I am so weak.

The most natural beauty in the world is honesty
and moral truth. For all beauty is truth.
—LORD SHAFTESBURY

Chapter Eight

We've been in Kristen's bedroom for nearly two hours getting ready for Amber's party. Actually, that's not entirely true. I've been getting ready for about forty-five minutes. The rest of that time has been spent calming Kristen down and trying to convince her to eat something. She hates eating before she goes out, but I promised her mother I'd make sure she did. And I'm not in the business of letting her mother down. It'd be like letting my own mother down.

"You've got to eat something," I tell her. "Your mom will kill me if I let you go hungry."

Kristen closes the eyelash curler and looks at me in the mirror. "I'll eat in a second. But I can't eat much. If I eat too much, I'll bust right out of this dress. I swear I've gained five pounds since we bought this."

I put a small plate of Wheat Thins and cheese in front of her. "I'm telling you right now. If you don't eat, you don't go.

I know all your little tricks. You stall and stall and then—
bam!—your date is here and you don't have time to eat. Fast-
forward two hours and three beers later and you can barely
stand. Is that really how you want Rock to see you?"

She sighs, tossing a cracker and cube of cheese into her
mouth. "I'm probably not going to drink, anyway. Not unless
he does."

I shake my head, more to myself than anyone. I hate that
she works so hard to please the guy in her life. She'll completely change herself if necessary. She deserves someone who
will love her just as she is.

"What time is it?" she asks, popping another Wheat Thin
before tossing her hair over her head, shaking it loose, and
then throwing it back over her shoulders.

I glance at my phone. "Eight forty. He's ten minutes late."

"Good thing," she says with a wink. "Otherwise I wouldn't
have had time to eat."

Kristen sprays her neck with perfume, then turns to
face me.

"Wow," I say. "You look phenomenal. Really."

"You too, Sarah. That shirt is perfect."

I glance in the mirror and look at us side by side. Kristen
looks like Red-Carpet Barbie and I look more like College-Prep
Barbie. I'm saved from second-guessing my outfit when the
doorbell rings.

Kristen flies out of the room, unplugging the hair dryer
and straightener in one swift motion. "That's him!"

I follow behind her with the half-empty plate of cheese

and crackers and set the dish on the kitchen counter while Kristen opens the door to Rock.

"Hey, gorgeous," he says to her, all deep and gravelly.

I walk into the living room, where they're standing in the doorway admiring each other.

"I'm ready," I announce, grabbing my purse from the coffee table and following them out the door.

Rock's truck is detailed in the way that lets you know he spends a lot of time taking care of it. There isn't a single water spot on it and the tires are shiny, like they've just been polished.

I hoist myself into the backseat and sink into the comfortable leather. While Kristen and Rock playfully fight over the radio, I pretend to busy myself with my phone. I figure it's the best I can do in the short five-minute drive to Amber's house.

When Rock parks the truck on the road and turns off the engine, I open my door and literally fall out. The seats are so slick I completely lose my hold on the door handle and land on my knees.

"You okay?" Rock asks, extending his hand to me as Kristen chuckles.

"I'm fine," I insist, ignoring his hand and quickly standing. I brush off my jeans and give Kristen a good glare. "That'll be enough out of you."

She grabs my hand and pulls me next to her. "You know I love you."

"Yeah, yeah," I say, making no effort to hide my sarcasm.

Amber's parties are always in the backyard around her parents' custom-made pool. There are palm trees full of twinkling white lights and tiki huts set up around the sparkling blue water.

"Wow," Rock says. "It's like being transported to South Beach."

Before either of us can respond, Amber rushes over. Her dark red hair is pulled back neatly and her clothes, like always, are very country-club chic. She's been dressing like a thirty-something divorcée on the prowl for a golf-playing, bourbon-guzzling, moneymaking husband for as long as I can remember. Her parents have a time-share in Colorado and they go away for their anniversary the first weekend of September every year. When that tradition began, so did Amber's back-to-school party.

"I'm so glad you came, Rock!" Amber says. "And you were nice enough to bring Kristen and Sarah. As if you could ever separate those two. Let me introduce you to the guys." She walks away with her arm in Rock's like they're the freaking Kennedys.

Kristen steps back like she's been slapped, but Amber pulls Rock away so quickly she doesn't have time to respond.

"That bitch," Kristen mumbles under her breath.

"Ignore her. She's just being a good hostess."

Kristen levels a serious look at me. "How can someone so smart be so naive?"

"It's either that or sit around and be mad. We came to have fun, so let's get a drink and then walk around."

Squaring her shoulders, she nods and walks with me to the nearest tiki hut.

"What can I get you, Sarah?"

I turn to see who's talking to me and come face-to-face with Jay Thomas. "Hi, Jay."

"Can you believe this place?" he asks.

"It's over the top. Every year, they add more and more. Where do you go for vacation if this is your backyard?"

Jay laughs, the way I usually see him. "I fully expect to see this backyard on the cover of *Better Homes and Gardens* someday soon. Isn't this the kind of thing those uppity tea-party types go for?"

I point to the drink in his hand. "That's what we're looking for."

He slides behind the counter of the hut and puts a bright pink plastic cup in front of me, then smiles at Kristen. "Would you like a drink, too?"

"Definitely," she says. "No sense suffering while he's over there partying it up."

Jay artfully ignores Kristen, another thing she's not accustomed to. "What'd you do this summer?" he asks me as he fills our cups from the keg.

"Worked a little for Mom, hung out with Kristen. What about you?"

He shakes his head. "Nada."

Kristen nudges my elbow as she grabs her cup; it's her not-so-subtle sign we need to be on the move. But I'm not about to leave Jay so rudely.

"Can you believe Rock is chumming it up over there with Amber and her goons?" Kristen is in full-pout mode, eyes trained on Rock and Amber like they're trying to get away with something illegal, instead of playing a card game using peanuts as poker chips.

"You have *got* to relax. He's new to the school and she's helping him make friends. I know you find this hard to believe, but guys like having other guy friends. Give him space. Rock will find his way back over here. Promise."

"Yeah," Jay interjects. "Guys hate an insecure girl."

"I am *not* insecure!" Kristen stands straight, shoulders back, in an attempt to prove what she said.

I put my arm around her shoulders. "It's okay, sweetie. We're going to have a great time—with or without him."

She looks at me in disbelief. "Doing what?"

"Come on," Jay said. "A bunch of us are hanging around the fire pit. We could use some intelligent conversation. Till now, the deepest topic we've discussed is how many times Amber will be married before our tenth high school reunion."

Kristen smiles. "Million-dollar question, for sure."

We follow Jay to the small group of kids in lawn chairs around the fire. I have to admit, it looks totally relaxing in a summer-camp kind of way.

We say hello to Jay's friends—Pete, Vanessa, Travis, and Becca. We've gone to school together for years. We've been in a lot of the same classes but never really hung out together. They're the kids everyone likes. Fun, smart, and completely above the clique drama.

"Jay, what do you think? Who here is most likely to wind up on the TV show *Intervention*?" Pete asks.

Jay laughs. "That's easy. Amber's husband."

"Doesn't count," Vanessa says. "How do we know he's here?"

"Yeah, but we don't know he's not." Jay follows Kristen's gaze to where Rock is sitting. Amber is sitting across from Rock, leaning so far forward her chest is practically spilling onto the table between them.

Kristen snaps her attention back to the fire, as if she couldn't care less about Rock.

The next several hours continue along the same lines . . . Who will never get married? Who will be the first to marry? Who will have the most kids? Who is most likely to wind up on Capitol Hill?

A couple of times Rock's looked over his shoulder and tossed Kristen a wink or a smile. But he hasn't left the table once. And since he's been turning down beer all night, and Amber continues to bring him Cokes, he doesn't really have a need to leave the table.

But when the crowd starts dwindling and people start leaving the party, Rock stands, does a complicated fist-bump thing with the other guys at the table, and walks over to us. He's smiling from ear to ear and it's obvious he's had a great time, even if he didn't quite realize the storm brewing within Kristen.

"You gals ready to head home?" he asks.

I expect Kristen to launch into a *Fatal Attraction* tirade about how she didn't appreciate being ignored and brace myself for the fireworks. So maybe I won't have to say anything to her about Rock after all. Maybe it'll just self-destruct if I leave it alone.

"Only if you are," she answers sweetly, nearly causing me to pass out in shock.

I watch in stunned fascination as she slides her hand into his and walks with him back to his truck.

"Sorry I got caught up with those guys. Didn't want to turn down a good game of poker when I'd just met them."

"I understand. It's not a big deal," Kristen says gently. "Sarah and I were just fine."

"Thanks for being so cool." He stops at the passenger door of his truck and opens it for her. With one hand, he effortlessly helps her into the truck.

I'm standing beside him, watching the exchange carefully. To be honest, it's a little embarrassing to be witnessing it. This kind of cooing should really be done in private.

"We'll have more time to talk tomorrow," Rock says, leaning in to give her a kiss on the cheek before closing her door.

When he jogs to his side of the truck, hops inside, and starts the engine, I quickly jump in before he takes off without me.

For the first time in a long time, I feel utterly invisible.

Beauty is not caused. It is.
—EMILY DICKINSON

Chapter Nine

When we wake up the following morning close to eleven, Kristen's house is quiet. Her mom was asleep when we got home last night and is probably already gone. We've spent hundreds of weekends like this—moving between our houses based on who was home and what we wanted to do. Kristen has a pool, so we are here more often than not. The fact that we're usually here alone is just icing on the cake.

"Let's get some sun," she says, eyes still closed.

I sit up and my stomach growls. "Food, then sun."

"You first," Kristen says, rolling over in bed.

Pushing to my feet, I head for the kitchen, where I grab an apple out of the fridge, open the blinds, then take a bite. Kristen's backyard isn't as luxurious as Amber's but it's so much better in lots of ways. Nothing in this backyard is breakable and the furniture is comfortable and well used. The sunlight dances on the top of the water, practically begging us to jump in.

When I get back to the bedroom, Kristen's deep breathing tells me she's fallen back asleep. I take the covers and yank them off her. She despises it when I do that, but it's the only way to actually get her out of bed.

"Come on, Kris. You need to spend some time in the sun."

"I hate you," she mumbles in her pillow.

"Just think how much prettier you'll look tonight with freshly tanned skin. No one likes a pasty girl."

And that's all it takes to get her feet on the ground. In a matter of minutes, she's brushed her teeth and pulled her hair into a ponytail and is—barely—dressed in her skull-and-crossbones bikini.

We both jump into the pool to get wet before climbing out and taking our usual lounge chairs in the full blazing sun.

"Now, isn't this better than wasting the day in bed?" I ask.

"Actually, it's a lot like wasting the day in bed. I'm just in bed outside." Kristen giggles at herself. She keeps her eyes closed as she talks. "So tell me. What do you think about Jay?"

My mind slips back to the hours we spent cutting up with Jay and his friends last night. "He's nice enough. Funny as hell."

"I like a guy who can make me laugh," Kristen says, a smile creeping onto her face.

I smile back, ready for our favorite game. "I like a guy who doesn't say 'pull my finger.'"

Kristen laughs. "I like a guy who doesn't floss with used floss."

"Eww! I like a guy who doesn't cry at coffee commercials."

"I like a guy who doesn't put sweaters on his cat."

I laugh so hard, I start coughing. "Omigod, Kris. That's your best one yet."

She high-fives me. "Guess Jay's not the only funny one."

✦ ✦ ✦

Seven hours later, I'm watching Kristen suffer over each choice while getting dressed. It's a miserable way to spend any Saturday evening, but tonight it's downright agonizing.

"Choose a shirt already!" I say, amazed that it can actually take someone over an hour to choose a shirt.

Kristen looks at the pile of clothes heaped on her bed, all of which she's tried on and dismissed. Twice. "I seriously need to go shopping," she mumbles.

"We just did and you have more clothes on this bed than I have in my entire house. *Pick. Something.*"

"It has to be just right," she says, arms folded across her bra-covered chest. It's hard not to hate her when she looks like a model. When she still finds something to complain about, it's enough to make me consider strangling her. Just for a second, anyway.

"Go with the red. It's definitely your color."

"Too bold," she says.

"How about the white tunic? White's great with your tan."

She scrunches up her face. "Too . . . virgin."

I look at my watch. "It's seven. You've got half an hour. He's a guy, Kristen. The only thing he'll notice is what's *in* the shirt."

"Even Rock?"

90

"He's smart, Kristen. Not dead."

She nods her head, a smile finally creeping onto her face. "You're right. Of course you're right." She grabs the red shirt from the corner of the bed and pulls it over her head. I have to admit she looks stunning. If anyone should be on television spoon-feeding the breaking news to Houstonians, it's her. She's totally got the glamorous looks and style for that kind of thing.

Her phone beeps twice, the oft-heard signal that Kristen's got a text message. She grabs the phone from the bed and stands frozen while she reads. "Holy crap."

Kristen has a tendency to overreact. To everything. So it takes a lot for me to get alarmed. I don't even bother asking her what the problem is. At this point, all I can think about is getting out of here before Rock arrives.

"Ticktock," I say, urging her to snap out of it and focus on her date.

"Read this," she says, tossing me the phone. "Then reply for me."

I do this a lot for Kristen when she's driving, doing her nails, or just plain lazy. I turn the phone over in my hands and read the text she's opened on her iPhone.

I've been waiting to see you all day. Hope you don't mind if I'm early.

I swallow the lump in my throat, willing my face to look bored when what I'm really feeling is stripped of my very own happily ever after.

Kristen bends over and brushes her hair. "Are you replying?"

"What do you want me to say?"

She stands up, tossing her hair back. "Something cute, clever. Something funny."

"If it's so easy, why don't you do it?"

Hands on her hips, she faces me. "Because you're so good at it, Sarah. Please?"

I sigh, knowing I can't or won't say no. Tapping the screen to life, I click Reply and type the first thing that comes to mind.

Hope you don't mind that I've memorized your eyes.

I click Send and put the phone back on the bed. "I'm not doing that again."

"Sure you are," she says, grinning at herself in the mirror.

Another two beeps on the phone.

"What'd you say to him?" she asks, reaching for the phone.

"That you liked his eyes." I lie back on the bed and cover my eyes with my arm.

She giggles, then shakes my leg. "Listen to this. 'They could never compare to your own. They put the Hope diamond to shame.'"

"Sweet," I mumble, eyes still covered.

"But I don't get it. Isn't a diamond clear? I mean, my eyes are about as blue as they get. Clear eyes? Eew."

I shake my head. How can someone be seventeen, have

watched *Titanic* a dozen times, and not know the Hope diamond isn't a traditional diamond? Honestly.

"The Hope diamond is blue," I tell her, doing my best not to add something completely rude and sarcastic.

Kristen sighs like a dreamy girl from a second-rate fifties film. "He's perfect."

He *is* perfect . . . but for her or for me?

She puts the phone in her pocket, then grabs the straightener from her dresser. "Can you run this over the back? I can never really reach it."

I nod, wishing I was anywhere else. Like getting ready for my own date with Rock. I pull her already-straightened hair through the CHI while she scrutinizes her face in the mirror.

"Is it just me or is my chest splotchy?"

I don't have to look in the mirror to answer. "You always get like that when you're nervous, Kris." And the fact that she's nervous tells me she's really excited about Rock. I mean, completely over the top. Because she dates. A lot. And never gets nervous.

And in that little telltale sign, I know being a good friend to Kris is the right thing to do. Rock means a lot to her, to her happiness. What if he *is* the one for her?

She takes the oversized powder brush and dips it into her bronzing dust with just the right amount of sheen. Two swipes across her chest do the trick, easily camouflaging her one fault. "God, I hate when I get like this. You're so lucky you don't have to worry about this kind of thing."

I release her hair from the straightener and lean against the dresser so we're facing each other. "What do you mean?"

93

Eyes wide with realization, she starts backpedaling. "You know what I mean, Sarah. You're . . . um . . . you're lucky you don't get all splotchy like this."

Narrowing my eyes, I study her. In my heart, I know she would never intentionally hurt my feelings. But still. "Because it sounded like I don't have to worry about getting all dressed because I can't get a date." Which, now that I say it out loud, is completely accurate. So what's my point?

Kristen shakes her head emphatically, grabbing my hands and squeezing them. "You know that's not true," she says. "Honest. And you could date about a hundred guys. But you don't put yourself out there, you know?"

And I guess she's right. I've never really been up to the challenge. It's always been so much easier, so much safer, to pretend I don't want to date. I've never been able to take that leap and just give it the old college try, as Mom says.

"I'm sorry," I mutter, feeling 100 percent ashamed. "I'm just . . ." I trail off, not sure what to say. If I was up to telling the truth, I'd tell her what a jealous wench of a friend I am. But I won't spoil this night for her. No matter how bad it hurts.

I finally finish my sentence with a lame, "Forget I said anything."

Fortunately, she does and practically dives into her closet looking for shoes. She's tossing out possibilities when I catch a glimpse of myself in the full-length mirror hanging on her bedroom door. When I see myself like this, head on, I can almost visualize the face I'd have with a normal nose.

Almost.

Kristen snaps her fingers in front of me. "Hel-*lo*. Help!" She points to her feet, a black ballet flat on her right foot, dressy red sequined sandals with a tiny little kitten heel on the left.

"Definitely the red," I say.

"But my toes are painted hot pink."

"Get the polish," I sigh. "I'll paint them for you while you put on your jewelry."

Kristen tosses me the red polish on her dresser and reaches for the silver heart necklace she reserves for special occasions. Against her bronzed chest, it looks incredible.

Just as I finish the last toe, the doorbell rings.

"Omigod," she whispers loudly, like he might be able to hear us outside. "That's got to be him."

I look at the clock, then back at Kristen. "Five minutes early. That's more like it."

I screw the lid on the polish and return it to the dresser, then walk to the window to peek outside. "I can't see him, but his truck's out front."

Kristen's mom opens the front door and invites Rock inside. It's easy to pick out his voice; the smooth, deep texture reminds me of melted chocolate.

"Come on, Kris. You look amazing." I grab her arm and pull her from the mirror and out of the bedroom. When we enter the living room, I'm struck speechless.

No guy has a right to look this freaking hot.

Just-right jeans with a sexy, black button-down shirt opened just enough to reveal a rope necklace.

"Hey, Sarah," he says, obviously surprised to see me. "You joining us tonight?"

"Oh, no. I was just leaving," I say, reaching for my purse on the coffee table.

"Hi, Rock." Kristen eases into the room, working her way around me to get closer to her date. "You met my mom?"

"Oh, yeah, we've already met," Kristen's mom says, all smiles. I can hardly blame her. Shoot, a nun would be smiling at this guy. "I guess you two better get shaking if you're going to make it there by eight. You know how traffic can be."

"It was nice meeting you, Mrs. Gallagher." Rock reaches forward to shake her hand and I can tell she's impressed. Who wouldn't be?

When Rock opens the door for Kristen, I walk out behind her, seriously regretting that he's following me in my old Levi's and last year's football T-shirt. I'm quick to flee his line of sight by walking across the lawn to my car, which is parked nose to nose with Rock's truck.

My car is actually Mom's old Lexus, black with tinted windows. Very mysterious looking, which is totally not my personality, but I love it anyway.

"Sarah," Rock says, stopping at the end of the sidewalk.

"Yeah?" I ask, fully aware that Kristen's waiting for him to open her door but watching me.

"Why don't you come with us?" he asks, smiling like he isn't asking me to do the utterly impossible.

"Oh, no, no. I couldn't. I'm busy, busy, busy. Y'all have fun." I click the unlock button on my car remote, frantic to escape. I'd rather walk on fire than be the third wheel on their date, watching them snuggle, feed each other, hold hands. And, what, I get to witness their kiss good night? No freaking way.

"That's crazy," he argues, oblivious to the daggers Kristen's shooting his direction. "There's plenty of room, right, Kristen?"

She pastes a toothy pageant-queen smile on her face and nods at Rock, then at me. "Of course," she says, but her eyes are conveying an entirely different meaning.

"Maybe next time." I open my car door and slide inside. As I start the engine, Rock walks to the passenger side of the truck and opens the door for Kristen.

I quickly tap my horn as I pull away from the curb, wishing like hell I actually had something to do besides think about him.

+   +   +

When I pull into our driveway, I notice Mom's car in its usual spot in the garage and a sporty red convertible I don't recognize parked by the curb. After parking behind Mom, I walk into the house and find her and Jen sitting at the kitchen bar.

"Hi, honey," Mom says. "You remember Jen, don't you?"

Remember her? It was only two days ago. "Sure. It's good to see you again."

Jen gives me a camera-worthy smile and I feel immediately second class. Next to Jen's to-die-for ivory pantsuit, I look downright destitute.

"We're just having a little after-work chat," Mom says, a

flush on her cheeks that was no doubt put there by the red wine. Judging from the empty bottle on the counter, they've been chatting a while.

"Girl night. Got it." I grab a bottled water from the fridge before kissing her on the cheek. "I'm headed to my room. I've got some research to do."

"On a Saturday night?" Jen asks, pity marring her impeccable features. "When I was your age . . ."

"Not my Sarah." Mom's practically misty eyed. Damn wine always makes her emotional. "She's such a good girl. Always so responsible."

"Sure, Mom," I say, walking out of the kitchen and up the stairs to my room.

When I sit on the bed to kick off my shoes, I notice a new brochure sitting on my nightstand. I grit my teeth, frustrated that Mom doesn't understand this is a closed subject. But as I walk to the trash can to lay it to rest, the title catches my attention.

Why Not Find Out What Plastic Surgery Can Do for You?

It's that simple; nothing else is written on the front except for that question. Naturally, the requisite picture of an absolutely gorgeous couple is front and center, all smiles with whitened teeth and the best little noses money can buy.

I open the brochure and scan through the same rhetoric inside every plastic surgeon's ads. Still, something about this one has me intrigued, so I open my laptop, connect to the

Internet, and type in the website address. I roll my eyes at myself, seriously thinking I need therapy. Never before have I actually researched a plastic surgeon, not that I'm really doing that now. But still, before Rock came along, I wouldn't have given it a second thought.

But maybe it's not just about Rock. Maybe it's just . . . time.

I'm not a naturally ambivalent person. Being decisive is one of the things I like most about myself. But when it comes to my nose, I just can't make myself stand steadfast in one decision for very long. I guess I have the right to be conflicted at seventeen.

When the website pulls up, there are even more pictures of pretty people. Flashing in the right-hand corner is a red circle; on the inside it reads "Why Not?"

I click the circle, which takes me to a page where I can load my picture, which I do quickly when I realize what this site offers: the ability to give my face a new nose, even if it's only in a picture.

With last year's school picture on the screen, I study the different noses available. There are about a million different choices. Who knew there were so many different shapes and sizes? Geez, talk about a tough decision.

I start with the one that looks most like Kristen's, which I've always considered God's best handiwork. But on me, the nose looks positively puny. I mean, maybe I'm just used to seeing myself with this oversized sniffer, but it totally doesn't fit me.

The next nose I click is a little longer, but still well within the normal limits as far as noses go. It definitely looks better than the first one, turned up just a little, and not too wide for my face.

I print the picture and lay it next to my laptop. It looks good, real good. But it's still so different from what I'm used to. It's just not . . . me.

Rubbing my hand over my nose, I try to imagine what it'd be like to go to college completely normal. With nothing freakishly large plastered on my face. A fresh start where no one would know the old me, the old nose. There would be nothing to stop me from doing or being whatever I want. No excuses.

As I'm about to close the website, I see a button that reads "Watch Us at Work" and click it. A video begins playing and the screen is filled with images of some poor schmuck with half his face peeled back. I have to stop myself from upchucking what little I've eaten today. It's beyond gross.

Someone narrates the rhinoplasty procedure like what they're doing isn't the nastiest thing ever. Shuddering, I close the window and slam the laptop closed.

Picking up the picture of me with a new nose, I think of the video. Good as the new nose looks, it'll be a cold day in hell before I let someone butcher me like that.

I wad up the picture and toss it into the trash, thankful I finally came to my senses before I did something foolish.

No object is so beautiful that, under certain conditions,
it will not look ugly.
—OSCAR WILDE

Chapter Ten

Just after midnight, my cell phone rings, pulling me out of a deep sleep. I seriously consider ignoring it, but I know it's Kristen from the unfamiliar tune screaming at me. She has a really bad habit of changing my ringtone for her. Of course, she never tells me when she's done that, so it's always a surprise. Her choices are superobscure: usually oldies because she knows I love them. This time, I'm treated to the theme song from *The Golden Girls*, "Thank You for Being a Friend." I should recognize the tune easily enough; it's one of Mom's favorite shows.

I reach for the phone, because she'll just keep calling until I answer. I've tried to dodge her long-winded late-night calls before and nothing works. She's like a dog with a bone.

"This better be good," I grumble into the phone.

"Omigod, Sarah," she squeals, the high pitch shooting through my ears straight to my brain. "It's about a gazillion times better than good!"

I roll over and turn on the lamp. There are at least a thousand other things I'd rather do than listen to Kristen recount every last sordid detail of her night with Rock, but this is our postdate routine; there's no changing it now. And deep inside, there's a sick part of me that almost *wants* to hear it all, like the car wreck you don't want to see but can't stop looking at.

"Tell me all about it," I say.

"Well, first of all, his hands are freaking amazing," she gushes, like I don't already know. Like the memory of those hands doesn't torture me. Especially now, knowing she's felt them, too.

"Uh-huh," I mumble, eyes closed.

"I mean, they're like totally huge and, omigod, they're so soft." She pauses abruptly. "But you already know that, don't you," she whispers, more to herself than to me, disappointed she wasn't the first one to hold his hand.

"So tell me something I don't know," I say, further proof I'm a glutton for punishment.

"Okay," she says, the excitement back in her voice. "So we're at the restaurant and while we're waiting, we check out some of the fish. That's when he put his arm around my waist. And it was so natural, like we'd been together forever."

I nod, knowing she can't see me but unable to actually form words. It makes my stomach churn to think about the two of them together. And just hearing her echo my own thoughts about how easy it is to be with Rock is like a sucker punch in the gut.

She ignores my silence. "It was supercrowded, so we had to

wait for over an hour. And you know how long it takes to eat at that place. We were there almost two hours and there wasn't a single awkward silence. Not one!"

"No *David Copperfield* discussions?" I ask.

Kristen laughs softly. "No, I did exactly what you said and kept the conversation personal. It worked like a charm."

"Good to know." I'm the most loyal friend on the planet, hands down. And quite possibly the biggest idiot.

"When we got home, we sat in his truck for a few minutes, then . . ." She draws out the word "then," doing her best to ramp up the drama. Like I don't know what's coming next.

"Then he *kissed* me. Not just a sweet peck on the lips. It was the kind of kiss that actually made me weak in the knees. I didn't even know what that meant before last night."

Of course he kissed her. I mean, I didn't really expect the night to end with a handshake, but hearing her say it out loud makes it real. Painfully real.

The last thing I want is to hear the details of the killer kiss to end the night of all nights. "Don't need the specifics, Kristen," I say, trying to hold it back but knowing it's totally useless.

"It was just perfect, Sarah. Totally, completely, 100 percent perfect."

"Perfect," I echo.

+ + +

I'm sitting on the couch at ten the following morning and watching a documentary on the role of journalism in the wake of 9/11 when the doorbell rings. And rings. And rings.

This is one of the Sundays that Mom works, so I'm home alone. I pause the show, then half jog to the front door and look out the peephole, where I see Kristen smiling and waving, a brown paper sack dangling from her dainty fingers. I know that sack.

I open the door and she flies inside, whipping past me. "Hungry? I brought your favorite," she says.

"My favorite?"

"Cinnamon-crunch bagel from Panera." She tosses the bag to me and looks me up and down. "Still in your pj's?" she asks.

"Sue me."

She waves her hand dismissively. "No time. I need your help."

"Of course you do," I mumble.

Kristen grabs the remote and turns off the television. "Rock friended me on Facebook."

"I was watching something," I say, pointing at the black screen of the television.

"This is way more important than some documentary. Geez, bor-ing."

"All you have to do is confirm him as a friend, Kristen. It's not rocket science. You've done it a thousand times." I grab the remote from her hand and swiftly turn the television back on. I set the remainder of the show to record, then turn the television off.

"I know *that*," she says. "But you don't expect *me* to write him, do you?"

Shaking my head, I laugh. "You've lost it."

"It's not funny, Sarah," she whines. "I mean it. Once I confirm him as a friend, he's going to want to talk there, too. What if I say something wrong?"

I sit on the couch next to Kristen and grab her hands. "This is ridiculous, Kris. You can't go through an entire relationship faking it. It's wrong, not to mention unnecessary. Rock already likes you."

"Because he thinks I'm smart!"

"And kind and pretty and funny."

"Please, Sarah. You don't have to do it forever, just . . . just for a little while."

"What are you going to do? Run over here every time he sends you a Facebook message?"

"I've thought it all through," she says, pride lighting her face. "I'll give you my sign-on information and you can log on from here and write him back and forth. Then when you're done, I'll just go back and read what y'all talked about so I'm not lost."

The absurdity of it has my head swimming.

"Hel-*lo*?" Kristen snaps her fingers to get my attention. "Did you hear what I said?"

I nod slowly. "I think I heard you say that you want me to write to him on Facebook as you."

"Right!"

"You want me to log on to your Facebook account and reply to his messages as if I'm you and keep that conversation going . . . without your input."

"Exactly," she says, nodding her head in satisfaction.

"This doesn't strike you as the tiniest bit deceitful?"

"Of course not! It's not like you're hacking into my account. I'm giving you my sign-on. You totally have my permission."

I stay silent, unsure what to say, knowing that nothing will change her mind. And until I agree, she'll make my life miserable.

"You're the only one I trust," she says. "We'll confirm him right now, then I'll text you when he sends a message so you can log on and get busy writing. Okay?"

She mistakes my silence for agreement. "I love you!" With a quick hug, she jumps off the couch and heads up the stairs to my bedroom and my laptop.

I look quietly at the space where Kristen sat, seriously contemplating a mad dash to the car. Of all the mind-numbing schemes she has roped me into, none of them put me at risk of getting hurt. Not like this.

"Sarah!" Kristen screams over the balcony. "I need you to unlock the laptop. Pronto!"

Blowing hair out of my eyes, I stomp up the stairs like a grouchy child. When I walk into my bedroom, Kristen's sitting on the bed, laptop open to the log-in screen. I sit down next to her, grab the computer, and reluctantly type in my password.

"Happy?" I grumble.

"Yes, yes, yes!" In a span of three seconds, she logs on to Facebook and confirms Rock as a friend. I manage to sneak a peek at his profile picture and instantly wish I hadn't. Seeing his face churns the dread settled in the pit of my stomach.

"Okay," Kristen says, eyes glued to the computer screen. "Let's see what happens."

"Chill. It's not like he's just sitting at the computer waiting for you to confirm him," I say, grabbing the bagel from the bag and picking off the crusty sweet cinnamon from the top. My favorite breakfast, hands down. Kristen knows all my weaknesses.

"Omigod!" Kristen shouts, scaring me so badly I lose my grip on the bagel. "He sent me a message. Look, look!"

Already? Maybe he *was* waiting for her reply. My heart immediately jumps into overdrive and I take a deep breath to steel myself for the words I'm about to read. I lean closer to read Rock's message.

Good to hear from you, gorgeous. I had a great time last night. Since we only have one class together, I propose we start a round of Twenty Questions, a game my family played on road trips. Actually, we still play it. The way it works is I'll send you a question, you answer, then ask your own question.

I'll start.

If you had one day left in this world, how would you spend it?

In spite of the fear splayed across Kristen's face, I grin. It's an awesome question and I would love to know Rock's answer.

I picture him somewhere quiet with his family. Maybe reading or writing or something equally peaceful at the edge of the lake, wearing nothing but swim trunks, his dark skin soaking up the summer sun . . .

"Um, that's supereasy. Shopping." Kristen smiles triumphantly.

My head snaps sideways, trying to focus on Kristen because that's who this is about. Not me. "Come again?"

"Shopping. What else is there?"

"Well, considering this would be your *last day on Earth*, I'm not sure shopping is the best use of your time. You'll only have a day to enjoy what you bought."

"That's the beauty of it; charge all day with no regrets," she says with a wink. "But I get your point. I guess I'd do something with you and my mom."

I pull the laptop from Kristen and reread the question to myself. "What do you really want to say?" I ask.

"I don't *have* a good answer, Sarah. Just write what you would do. I'm sure whatever it'll be he'll love it."

"You can't be serious," I tell her, eyes narrowed in disbelief.

"Of course I'm serious. Now get busy," she says, snapping her fingers playfully. "I'll grab you a Diet Coke while you play me."

I watch Kristen skip—yes, skip—out of the room.

Feeling like a total fake, I study the blank screen for what seems like an eternity before finding the words. My words.

I love these kinds of games. I'm in.

I've actually thought about this question a lot and my answer is pretty simple. Nothing too extravagant, too flashy. If I only had one day left to live, I would take my closest friends and my mom and spend the day at the beach in Kauai. Mom took me there when I was younger and it was the most beautiful, most relaxing place I'd ever seen. My only caveat is that I want a full twenty-four hours there, so my day starts after I get off the plane.

Now for my question . . . What is the worst thing someone has ever done to you?

Tag, you're it!

Love, Sarah

"Wait!" Kristen screams from behind me. I hadn't even heard her come into the room, so I nearly have a heart attack.

"Geez, are you trying to kill me? You scared the crap out of me." I lean back on the bed and take a deep breath. "What's the problem?"

"Hel-*lo*! You signed *your* name, doofus!"

I turn my eyes back to the screen and stare in shock at my mistake. "This is exactly why we shouldn't be doing this."

"It's fine," she says. "Quick fix. Just change the name and send it."

I glance over my words again, then click Send before I come to my senses.

And that one little click, something I've done a million times before, feels like I hammered the first nail in my own coffin.

✦ ✦ ✦

Jacobi booms like he's announcing the president of the United States. "Today marks a new beginning. Today, we will begin our study of one of the most tortured love stories ever written. *The Scarlet Letter* is timeless, a lesson in regret, in morality, in love." He finishes with a loud clap of his hands. "Let's get started."

I open my copy of the novel, a little bubble of excitement bouncing around in my chest. There's nothing I love more than the anticipation of starting a new adventure. Even if it's in a classroom. I know, I'm a total geek.

As I read along with Jacobi, I grow increasingly frustrated. Not by the book, but by my hair. I let it dry naturally this morning, so it's a little out of control, loose and curly, hanging in my face as I try to read, forcing me to spend half my time pulling it back and holding it out of the way. I finally twist my hair and use a pencil to hold it in place.

"Stop fidgeting with it. It's fine," Rock whispers from behind me.

His warm breath tickles my neck and I look over my shoulder to face the grinning god known as Kristen's boyfriend. "What?"

"Your hair."

I shrug, refusing to let a single kind word settle itself in my heart.

"Your assignment today is a paired discussion," Jacobi announces after he closes his tattered copy of the novel.

"We're partners, right?" Rock asks, like I'd actually consider pairing up with anyone else. It may be pure and utter torture, but what the hell. Sign me up.

I nod without turning around to face him. The last thing I need is for Jacobi to catch me not paying attention again.

"Your assignment is to discuss the quotes I give you. With your partner, I expect you to dissect the quote and talk about its meaning, its implication in the story. I also want you to think about whether or not the quote is relevant in today's society. Please get in your pairs and get to work."

I grab the pencil from my hair before turning to face Rock.

When Jacobi hands Rock our quotes, I lean forward in an attempt to read them upside down. Hawthorne's writing isn't as hard to understand as Shakespeare's, but one of the things I've learned from being in Jacobi's class is that he doesn't accept pat answers.

Rock shifts the paper so I can see it better and then reads the first quote aloud. "One token of her shame would but poorly serve to hide another."

He reads it with the ease of a college professor, with the exact intonation and meaning rarely heard from the lips of a high school senior. Especially a guy. When he reads the second quote, my eyes are shamelessly fixed on his face, his lips.

"Ah, but let her cover the mark as she will, the pang of it will be always in her heart."

Lord have mercy.

Kristen is the luckiest girl that ever lived. Honest to God.

"So," Rock says, breaking up my mental pity party. "Want to start with the first one?"

I nod, then look back at the quote. Anything but back into those mind-melting, heart-stopping, deep brown eyes.

One token of her shame would but poorly serve to hide another.

"What do you think?" he asks.

"Seems like he's trying to say you can't ever really hide your mistakes."

Rock nods, studying my face and making me feel completely uncomfortable. Still, I watch him watch me, looking for any telltale sign that he's studying my nose. But he doesn't. I swear he's looking into my eyes.

"Yeah," he says solemnly. "The scarlet letter isn't the only evidence of her mistake. There's still her daughter."

"Makes sense. Think it's true today?" I ask.

Rock bites his lip in a seriously enticing way, making me wonder exactly how he kissed Kristen. Did he hold her face? Did he put his hands in her hair as he brought her face to his? I fight the burn of tears in my eyes. Talk about a tortured love story.

"In a way," he says. "Not exactly like Hester's situation. Girls get pregnant all the time and don't get married. It's not considered a sin to have sex out of marriage these days."

Just the mere mention of sex sends a heat to my face I can't hide. What am I? Twelve?

In an effort to detract from my own scarlet display, I tag his thoughts with mine. "But I think, in a lot of ways, what he's saying is still true. I mean, we all make mistakes, but it's almost impossible to hide them. *Really* hide them."

"You're right," Rock agrees. "Definitely true. When I first got my license, I was backing up one foggy morning and hit my dad's car. Dented it all to hell."

"Uh-uh," I say, shaking my head, a smile creeping onto my face. I can just picture a younger Rock in full panic. "What'd you do?"

"I thought I could lie my way through it. Took off before Dad came out and then acted surprised when he told me about it that night."

"Get out."

"Serious. Of course, he'd known the second he'd laid eyes on the dent. He strung me along for a couple of days, building up the cost of the body work that had to be done. I was sweating like a heroin addict in detox."

"You finally spilled your guts?" I ask, laughing.

He shrugs. "Eventually I figured out he knew, so there wasn't any sense hiding it anymore. When he told me the paint from my green truck left a ten-inch mark on the side of his white car, I couldn't believe I'd been so stupid."

"It's amazing what we let ourselves believe." I'm a shining example.

"You'd never do anything that stupid," he says with a smile.

"You have no idea," I mutter. But we're not even going to get into how stupid I can be.

Rock turns the paper back so he can see it better, then rereads the second quote. "Ah, but let her cover the mark as she will, the pang of it will be always in her heart."

"You first," I say.

"It's about living with your choices, good or bad."

"Hester made a horrible choice."

"For the right reasons," Rock adds quickly.

"Which makes it even more heartbreaking. Knowing you did the wrong thing for the right reason doesn't go far in making you feel any better."

"You don't think?" he asks, searching my face again. And this time, he does it. His serious eyes settle on my nose and my heart sinks.

"No," I say, moving my head so we're face-to-face. Head on, my nose always looks smaller. I should know—I've studied it from every possible angle.

"Explain," he says, eyes back on mine. And it surprises me when he doesn't apologize or offer some lame comment about my "distinctive" nose, like everyone else.

"About a year ago, I was picking up some things at the grocery store. There was this woman in the same aisle as me and I could tell she was poor, maybe homeless. Her son pulled a jar of peanut butter off the shelf and tried to open it, but she took it from him and put it back on the shelf. He started crying about how hungry he was, so she picked him up and hugged him close, whispering something in his ear. I looked away to get what I needed and when I turned back around, I watched her put that jar of peanut butter in her purse. When she saw me, I could tell she was scared, you know? Worried I was going to rat her out. But I just smiled and walked to the check-out stand. I never said anything to anyone about that. Not even Mom, now that I think about it. That event's been ingrained in my mind. The pain and guilt in that mother's eyes haunted my dreams for months afterward. It breaks my heart to think that's someone's reality."

"Wow," he says softly.

"So doing the wrong thing—like my not reporting her or her taking the peanut butter—still makes you feel bad, even when you do it for the right reason."

"Point made," he says, then reaches up and rubs my arm in a move of total compassion. The warmth of his hand on me freezes me in place. Never before have I been affected by some-one's touch like this.

Never.

+ + +

On the way to lunch after lit, I do my best to keep the conver-sation with Rock light. Casual. Like I'm okay with him kissing my best friend.

And I must do a pretty good job, because the second we see Kristen waiting for us outside the cafeteria, he takes two big steps toward her, leaving me behind.

I can't pull my eyes away from the train wreck taking place right in front of me.

Rock reaching for Kristen, taking her hand.

Rock leaning close and whispering something in her ear.

Rock pulling her in for a quick hug.

It's more than I can stomach, and I turn to escape. But I'm not quick enough.

"Where do you think you're going?" Rock calls out, hand in hand with Kristen, proving he's still a guy and completely unaware of how agonizing this is for me.

I stop in my tracks and turn to face him. "Um . . ."

"Come on," Kristen says, smiling bright enough to burn my fair skin. "You have to eat."

I follow the embarrassingly happy couple into the cafeteria, wishing like hell I'd been smart enough to think of somewhere else to be. I mean, I'm about as tough a girl you'll ever find, but this is enough to wear me down.

By the time we make it to the table, I've totally lost my appetite. I do my best to play the supportive friend, like I'm happy to see Kristen in such obvious bliss. And it's not that I don't want her to be happy; I totally do. Always have, always will.

I was taught that friends are the most important people in your life because you get to choose them. Mom's words.

Mom never really had a best friend. Not as an adult, at least. She said she got burned by a friend when she first started in journalism and it must have been a scorcher, because the memory of that betrayal has kept her from trusting other women ever since.

She always taught me to take care of my friends. "Good friends you can trust are rare," she says. And she's right, of course. The hallways of this building are littered with superficial girls interested only in themselves. And they'll claw their way right over you to get what they want, regardless of who gets hurt in the process. I don't want to be that person to Kristen, the kind of person who would turn on her best friend, who'd throw away a lifelong friendship for selfish reasons.

Kristen and I have always stuck together.

Nothing's beautiful from every
point of view.
—HORACE

Chapter Eleven

Despite the fact I'm surrounded by more than fifty kids in the library, I don't have to turn around to know Kristen's walking up behind me. The floral scent of her perfume is the only announcement I need. Well, that and the energy radiating off of her. It's like having the sun at your back.

"Sit down," I say, never raising my eyes from the Emily Dickinson book opened on the old chipped table in front of me. I definitely don't want any trouble with our cranky librarian, Mrs. English.

Kristen takes two quick hops and practically bounces in the seat. "Put the book down," she whispers, yanking it from my hands and slamming it shut.

"Rude," I growl.

"Necessary," she singsongs, eyes dancing like a toddler who's just been given her first dollhouse. "It's e-mail–writing time."

I'm shaking my head before she finishes. It was bad enough

I did it once and brought them closer together. Then add the texting and Facebook . . . it's gone too far already. "N. O."

"Whatever," she says, totally dismissing me, which makes me even more resolute.

"I'm serious, Kristen. This is wrong. What if he finds out?"

"How would that ever happen? Are you planning to tell him?" she asks, arms crossed over her chest sullenly.

"Hardly," I scoff.

"Then what's the problem? What he doesn't know won't hurt him."

"Something tells me he might disagree."

Kristen turns her attention to the last page in her math folder. She shoves it in front of me ceremoniously, like she's just presented me with the winning lottery ticket.

I refuse to look down at the notebook, choosing instead to nail her with a deadly serious this-isn't-happening look.

She huffs a deep breath, and I think she's finally getting the point.

"I can't do it," I say quietly, casting a quick glance at Mrs. English sorting books on the library cart.

Kristen's frustrated expression is replaced with pleading blue eyes and a gut-wrenching look of panic. "You have to, Sarah. Please."

I pull the Dickinson book back in front of me and flip through the pages to find where I'd left off. "I don't have to do anything."

She grabs my hands and squeezes tightly. "Of course, you're right. You don't *have* to. But I know you will."

"Oh yeah?" I ask, half laughing.

"We do everything for each other. And besides, it's not like anyone will ever know except you and me."

"That's the problem, Kris. *I'll* know."

"Come on," she whispers, leaning closer. "I can't do this without you. Just read what I wrote and help me fix it. I'll e-mail it myself."

When she pushes the notebook closer, I finally allow my eyes to wander to the full page of writing. To say I'm surprised at the amount of writing she's done would be an epic understatement.

Raising my eyebrows, I look up at her. "You wrote this?"

She nods excitedly, knowing she's got me. Again. "What can I say? He's pretty inspirational."

Tell me about it.

Dear Rock,

Before I met you, I thought all guys were the same. They all want the same thing (and we both know what that is). But you are so different. You like to do different things, like talk and read and learn new things. That's totally cool. Don't get me wrong, I really liked the way you held my hand and kissed me. Really, really liked it. But I like talking to you and can't wait to go to the Museum of Fine Arts with you this weekend.

XOXO,

Kristen

A jolt of jealousy shoots through me. They're going to *my* favorite museum in Houston.

"Who's on display at the museum?" I ask. Even though I already know, I'm curious if she has a clue.

"Rock said impressionists, which I thought sounded totally cool. I mean, I love it when Jay Thomas does his impression of Napoleon Dynamite. Hilarious!"

My eyes fix on Kristen's, disbelieving. "Excuse me?" I whisper.

"Oh, come on. You've seen him do that a million times."

I wave my hand in front of her face. "That's not what I mean. Think about what you're saying, Kristen. You're going to a fine arts museum. To see impressionists."

Worry wrinkles the taut skin on her forehead. "Oh no," she says, slapping her hand over her mouth. "Omigod, Sarah. What was I thinking?"

It takes everything inside me to keep a straight face.

"It's not funny, Sarah! I went on and on about how my parents took me to see a famous impressionist when I was little."

"What was his name?" I ask.

"Rich something," she mumbles.

"Rich Little?"

"That's it!" She smiles happily, briefly forgetting how badly she's embarrassed herself.

"Impersonator, not impressionist," I tell her.

She swallows visibly. "I'm going to be sick."

"You told Rock about seeing Rich Little?" I ask, guessing I'm 100 percent right by the look on her face.

Kristen nods, her angelic face breaking into an adorable, embarrassed grin. "He just laughed like he always does, so I thought he was agreeing with me."

I can't stand for her to be so miserable. There is something inside me that makes me completely incapable of letting her stay that way. Reaching across the table, I rub her hand. "It'll be fine. I'm sure he thought you were just joking."

"You think?" she whispers.

"Positive," I answer with fake enthusiasm. "Let's check out this letter." Because, let's face it, there's no way I can refuse now. I don't have the heart to back out on her when she needs me so badly.

I scan the words again before taking a deep breath to speak quietly across the table that separates us. "Well, it's definitely better than the last one."

She nods, the frown of a few short seconds ago replaced with a self-satisfied smile that would make Miss America proud. "You can say that again."

I reread the first couple of lines. "I like your first sentence," I tell her honestly. Grabbing the pencil from my hair, I circle the sentence. "We can definitely keep that one."

"And the rest?" she asks. I can tell she's worried I'm going to tear it apart, revealing a rare insecurity, and my heart melts.

"Well, the message is really good, but we just need to reword it a little."

I pick up the notebook and walk to the computers, Kristen close on my heels. She's clapping her hands quietly behind me. "Thank you, thank you!" she nearly squeals, drawing a loud "Ssshhh" from Mrs. English.

When I pull out the chair to the only open computer, Kristen slides onto the chair with me. "Hover much?" I ask.

"There aren't any other seats," she complains.

After she signs on to her e-mail account, I pull the keyboard in front of me and stare at the blank e-mail filling the screen. I glance at the paper lying on the counter next to our computer and retype the first sentence, then let the words flow.

Straight from my heart.

Before I met you, I thought all guys were the same—shallow and self-centered. But you're nothing like that. You're intelligent, considerate, and generous. When you smile at me, it's like no one else exists and the world is reduced to just the two of us. There's so much I want to know about you and I'm going to treasure every minute of our time together. I don't know if it's the soft lighting or the artistic passion lining every wall, but there is something uniquely romantic about going to a museum together.

I do my best to lean back to study the screen and wind up squashing Kristen. But she's so completely caught up in what I've written she doesn't even notice.

"Oh. My. God." She squeezes me in a way-too-tight hug from behind. "You are freaking amazing, Sarah."

Shrugging my way out of the hug, I shake my head. "Not so much." If I'm so amazing, why can't Rock see it?

"How'd you know exactly what I was thinking?" she says, but doesn't wait for my answer. "Maybe I should study famous impressionists before our date."

"You'll be fine," I insist. But I wonder if I'm subconsciously setting her up, when she's so out of her element. Then I remember their meeting in front of the cafeteria and realize the museum will only serve as a beautiful backdrop for their unfolding relationship. Nothing more.

People like Kristen and Rock don't discuss art. They *are* art.

"Want to add anything else?" I ask, cursing myself for falling into this disaster again. The warm and fuzzy need to protect Kristen has been replaced by pity. Not attractive.

"Just my name," she says, reaching over and typing in the XOXO before her name.

I can't watch her click Send, knowing I'm just as deceitful as Kristen in this absurd scheme, so I make my way back to the table where I left my books.

If Rock ever finds out, we'll both be booted from his world.

✦ ✦ ✦

My cell phone is ringing when I walk into the house after school. I drop my backpack and purse on the floor before answering.

"Hello?"

"Sweetie, it's Mom. Can you do me a favor?"

"Depends," I say, wishing I'd let the call roll to voice mail. Mom's favors are never simple. The last time she asked me for a favor, I wound up standing in line at the DMV for over an hour.

She heaves a sigh of frustration, like I'm a total pain in her size-two pants. "What kind of answer is that?"

"An honest one," I reply, pulling a soda from the fridge.

"Very funny," she says, stern-mother voice piercing the phone line.

"What do you need?" I ask.

"Can you deliver dinner for me and Jen? And bring something for yourself, too. We'll eat together after the six o'clock."

"Late night?" I ask.

"Filling in for Lisa on the ten o'clock."

"Sure," I say, glad I don't have to cook. Normally, I wouldn't mind cooking, but this has been one of those days where I could totally use a break. "What do you want?"

"Cobb salads from Mama's Café."

"Dressing?"

"Just some lemon juice," she says. Mom says eating a salad with dressing is like having a Diet Coke with your double-patty burger and extra-large fries.

"On my way," I say, grabbing my purse from the floor and opening the front door as I end the call.

By the time I make it to the station, Mom's already in her seat behind the news desk and Vic has started the ten-second countdown. Mom gives me a small wink, then focuses her attention on the camera.

I quietly set down the bag containing our salads and cruise to my usual spot, ready to watch Mom in action. Just as Vic counts down from three, Jen blows through the door, grabbing everyone's attention. She offers an embarrassed wave and sits next to me as Mom assumes her newscaster persona on cue.

Jen leans close, hooking her arm with mine. "Call me crazy, but I love watching the news live."

I keep my eyes on Mom, a warm smile lighting her face. Feel-good story time. "Me, too."

"Especially your mom. She's amazing."

I nod, appreciating her recognition like a proud parent. "There's nothing like seeing her in action."

We watch in comfortable silence as Mom and David deliver Houston's headlines with a precision most often seen on the national news level.

"So, she's never been married?"

Instead of answering her, I put my finger to my lips in a useless attempt to quiet her.

"What about your dad?" she continues, eyes focused on me.

"He's never been around," I say, easily regurgitating the excuse I've used for seventeen years.

"That's too bad. She must get lonely."

My eyes move from Mom to Jen. "She doesn't have time to be lonely. You know what this job's like."

Jen shifts her attention back to the anchor desk, a serious look marring her beautiful face. "You'd think she'd want to move to a smaller market. Less hours, less stress."

I give Jen a look that lets her know exactly how insane that statement is. Mom would go nuts in a smaller market.

I've asked Mom why she never got married, but she says she married her job decades ago. There was never any room for a husband.

Jen squeezes my arm still looped in hers, sitting forward in her seat and dragging me with her. "My piece is coming up," she says excitedly.

I turn my attention to the big screen behind Mom and David, where Jen's *Vogue*-worthy face appears. The caption "Overcrowded Animal Shelter" is visible at the bottom of the screen.

"Oh my God, I look—" she begins, her face contorted as she studies herself.

"Amazing? Spectacular?" I softly fill in the blank with the obvious adjectives.

She looks at me like I've just told her I was naming my firstborn after her. "You're too sweet."

Jen watches herself on the screen, eyes drawn together critically. How in the world could she possibly think she looks anything less than gorgeous? It's obvious the camera loves her all-American looks, and her accent is just right for Texas. Not too northern, with a hint of southern charm. It's easy to see how she got tapped for a move from Texarkana to Houston after six months. She was born to be on-screen. In fact, she kind of reminds me of an older, brunette Kristen.

When the news wraps, Mom unclips her microphone and practically skips to where Jen and I are sitting. "My two favorite girls," she gushes. "Awesome piece today, Jen."

Jen smiles at Mom, clearly flattered. "Thanks, Beth. But I

think you might be right. It's time to add some highlights. My hair looked completely drab."

"Call Zander. Just tell him I sent you and he'll fit you in."

When I grab the take-out bag of salads, Mom wraps a thin arm around me, pulling me close in a way that I love. "How was your day, Sarah?"

"Fine," I say, giving her my usual nondescript answer.

She sighs impatiently. "That's all I get?"

"It was school, Mom. It's not like I went to the Grammys."

"Very cute," she says with a playful bump of her hip to mine as the three of us reach her office.

I place the bag on the large coffee table and unload the trio of salads, two with lemon juice, one with fat-free Italian. Settling into the overstuffed burgundy chair, I pull the lid off my salad and pour on the dressing. Lots of it.

"Sarah," Mom warns, hating that I won't jump on the lemon-juice-or-bust bandwagon.

"It's fat free," I say through a mouthful of salad.

Jen and Mom sit in the chairs opposite me in impossibly proper positions, like they're eating with the Queen of England.

"Don't you want to change clothes?" I ask.

"Still have another newscast," Mom says before turning her attention to her newest protégé. "Jen, tell Sarah about the scholarship."

"Oh yeah!" she says. "A while back, your mom told me you like to write. I love to write, too. That's what got me turned on to journalism in the first place. Anyway, I was research-ing a story on the rise in college tuition and the limited academic scholarships available to graduating seniors. That's when I found out another affiliate right here in Houston offers a five-thousand-dollar scholarship to journalism majors."

My eyes pop out in surprise. "It must be a new one, because I've never heard of it and I've done tons of research."

"It is; this is the first year," she says, salad still unopened. "I'll get you the forms. You have to write an essay. It should be a snap for you."

"Thanks," I say, grateful that someone like Jen is around. Not just for me, although I completely adore her, but for Mom.

Because it looks like she's *finally* got a friend she can trust.

Beauty is not in the face; beauty is a light in the heart.
—KAHLIL GIBRAN

Chapter Twelve

My phone signals a text message while I'm brushing my teeth the following morning. Mom is already back at work, so in the quiet of the empty house the bird-chirp tone is hard to miss, even with the water running.

I don't have to guess who it is, and I almost ignore it altogether, but curiosity gets the best of me.

Got a FB message from R. Do your thing.

I stare at the screen and consider my options. I can either log on and get it over with, or ignore the message until she guilts me into doing it two hours from now. Either way, I'm cornered. I click Reply.

You owe me.

Pulling my laptop from the nightstand, I bang my fingers on the keyboard to release some pent-up frustration. But if I'm totally honest, I'm anxious to see Rock's reply to my question. I realize he thinks he's talking to Kristen. Still, it's a brief, guilty glimpse into what it's like to be her.

I log on to Facebook and open the message from Rock to Kristen.

That was the best answer ever. I'll give you the flight time as long as you take me with you. I've never been to Hawaii but it's on my list of places to see before I die. I think my last day to live would be spent doing something similar, but it would definitely include fishing with my dad. I know some people would rather go skydiving or something equally dangerous, but where's the thrill when you know you're going to die in twenty-four hours? No, I'd rather spend that time with the people who mean the most to me.

Now for your question . . . You think *I* ask tough questions? Yours made me do some thinking about things I was trying to forget. Thanks for nothing. JK. The worst thing anyone has done to me has to be the time my best friend in Atlanta decided the only girl worth dating in our school of two thousand people was the girl I happened to be seeing. It destroyed our friendship. That's why I envy your friendship with Sarah; it's obvious she would do anything for you. That kind of friend is hard to find. Until my friend put me through that last year, I thought he was that kind of friend. But it just goes to show you never really know someone until things get tough or, in my case, you both want the same thing.

Next question: What is the first thing you notice about people?

See you tomorrow, gorgeous.

Even after I've read Rock's message three times, my pulse is sky high. The fact that he was hurt by someone stealing his girlfriend drives home the fact that I'm not near the friend he thinks I am. Or even the kind of friend Kristen thinks am I. That she *deserves*. If Rock—or, God forbid, Kristen— knew the reality of what I was actually feeling, I'd never be able to face either one of them. Add to that this deceitful little scheme Kristen's talked me into and I'm in full self- hate mode.

But at this point, I've gone too far to back out now. And in a totally twisted way, I love the chance to "talk" to Rock like his girlfriend, no matter how impossible that is. So with a healthy dose of disgust, I click Reply and, as Kristen puts it, do my thing.

It's hard to imagine you being vulnerable. For what it's worth, I think you're better off without the friend *and* the girlfriend.

Did I really just type that? I'm freaking talking about myself, for crying out loud! Ugh, I'm scum. Still, my scum-covered fingers get back to work.

The first thing I notice about people is their eyes. That's definitely the first thing I noticed about you, along with every other girl in the room. Especially when I saw you face-to-face. There was something in your eyes that captivated me . . . the color was definitely part of it, but it was more about the spark in your eyes. I could just tell you'd be someone I'd like, and I was right. Most people don't notice that about me, of course. It's hard to get to the eyes when there are much bigger things to notice about my face.

My question . . . guess I'll go easy on you this time. What song always makes you happy when you hear it?

Love, Kristen

Without rereading it, I click Send.
Second nail firmly secured in my self-created coffin.

✦ ✦ ✦

Monday morning, I pull the car to a stop in front of Kristen's house at seven thirty sharp, the dead weight of dread firmly rooted in the pit of my stomach. It's the same dread I woke up with this morning, knowing I'd be forced to face Kristen and the details of yet another romantic night she's shared with Rock. I'm seriously tempted to just peel out, burn rubber, and leave her to avoid it all.

By the time she finally bursts through the front door and races down the sidewalk, I've been waiting nearly fifteen minutes and we're running dangerously late for school, which just adds to the tension building within me. I'm strung so tight you could practically play me like a fiddle.

"Sorry, sorry, sorry," she gushes, snapping her seat belt in place. She's known me long enough to know I detest being late. The only thing I hate more is waiting on other people who are late.

"It's called an alarm clock," I say, doing my best to avoid looking at her. I can never stay mad at her when she gives me *the look*.

"We got home late last night," she says.

My throat tightens at the realization of what's coming. "Doesn't the museum close around six?"

Kristen turns in her seat and talks to my notable profile, something only she is allowed to do. "Well, we left there around five thirty, then we ate dinner at Pepper's Grill. I thought he was going to take me home, but he had something *amazing* planned."

Amazing. The word reverberates through my head, bringing on an instant massive headache. "Oh yeah?" I say, knowing there's no escaping the details when we're still five minutes from school.

"Get this," she says, hands out in front of her. "He took me to the Galleria and we went ice-skating. It was so wonderful. I mean, I'm a total klutz, so he was constantly grabbing me and picking me up. I'm telling you, Sarah, it was the most awesome date ever."

The vision of Kristen and Rock, hand in hand, arm in arm, laughing about her inability to stay off her butt is enough to shoot my headache into migraine status.

And I have only myself to thank.

+ + +

The next time I see Kristen is in journalism. Of course, she and Rock are practically making out in class, so I'm a total third wheel when I take my seat in the next aisle. Kristen looks up, smiling lazily, like she's in a love-induced haze. I guess if Rock was my boyfriend, I'd have a hard time keeping my hands and lips to myself, too.

"Hey," she says.

"How's it going?" Rock asks, turning the full effect of his attention on me. When he looks at me with those amazingly deep, sincere eyes, I have to remind myself he's Kristen's boyfriend and he's just being sociable.

I stare back at him, wishing like hell I had something incredible to say. Something that would make him wish he'd been with *me* last night. Something that would make him see he's e-mailing and Facebooking me, not Kristen.

Instead, I settle for a lame, "Pretty good. You?"

"Couldn't be better," he says with a wink in Kristen's direction.

Instead of attempting an answer, I simply nod while opening my notebook.

"Ignore her," Kristen says. "She's upset with me for making her late this morning."

"Not true," I quip, keeping my eyes on the notebook and trying to look like I'm reviewing my notes from last week.

"Whatever," she says, then turns her attention back to Rock. "Sarah hates it when I'm late. It makes her downright crazy."

My heart picks up its pace and my mouth fights to spew a few choice words Kristen's direction. How dare she air my faults? And, for the record, being punctual is so *not* a fault.

"My mom is the same way," Rock sympathizes.

Oh my God. Now I'm being compared to his *mother*?

Regardless of how badly I want to defend myself, I keep my mouth closed, not trusting the words that would fly out given half a chance. Getting into a fight with Kristen in front of Rock would not be cool.

Rock reaches over and pats my shoulder, like he's soothing a fussy preschooler. "I think it's great. I like being on time, too."

That gets my attention and I look up to see him smiling. I swear, his smile could light matches. It's that hot.

Before I can reply, Kristen turns in her seat to face me. "I've got it!" A shiver of dread slinks down my back. Declarations like this from Kristen are a bad omen. Every single time.

When I don't ask for details, she huffs a frustrated breath. "Don't you want to know?"

"Not particularly," I mumble, shaking my head, wondering what Rock makes of this exchange. Does he still see two best friends?

"Well, too bad. I'm telling you anyway," she says. "Why don't I start riding to school with Rock?"

A flush spreads across my chest and then my hands begin to shake.

She can *not* be serious. We have ridden to high school together every single day. I can't believe she's letting a guy—even one as stellar as Rock—come between us.

"I don't think that's going to solve your problem," I say, cursing the quiver in my voice.

"What problem? I don't have a problem," she says, 100 percent clueless that I'm fuming.

"The problem you have getting ready on time. At least I'm used to it. No need to make Rock late for school." Even as I say it, I know it's a lost cause. Kristen gets what she wants.

Period.

Rock clears his throat. "I don't mind driving you to school," he says to Kristen, "but I don't like the idea of breaking up your routine." The last sentence is directed straight at me, those damn probing eyes sending little rivers of heat through me.

Shaking my head, I focus on Kristen, ignoring the click of the door when Mrs. Freel shuts it behind her, signaling the beginning of class. "This is what you want?" I whisper to Kristen, shaky voice betraying the strength I'm attempting to exhibit.

"Well, sure," she says, confused. "This way, you don't have to ever wait on me and you'll be on time. I thought that's what you wanted."

I'm grateful Mrs. Freel begins speaking and keeps me from answering. Because, honestly, I would never tell her what I really want: that I want things to stay the same, that I don't want to be alone. I mean, the thought of walking up those stairs every morning without her beside me is terrifying.

More than anything, I just want my best friend back.

✦ ✦ ✦

After school, I stop at the grocery store and get some things for grilled tilapia. It's a beautiful day outside, the kind of day that screams backyard barbecue. And the last thing I need is to sit around with a bunch of idle time to obsess about Rock and Kristen.

I'm surprised when I turn onto our street and see a familiar red hot rod. Jen's convertible. But it's only five fifteen, so Mom definitely isn't home yet. I mean, that'd be a first. Maybe Jen and Mom went somewhere together. That would totally thrill me; Mom *needs* a lot more fun in her life. I've been telling her that for years.

After I pull into the driveway, I step out of the car, grocery bags in hand. Jen is leaning on the hood of her car, looking more casual than I've ever seen her in jeans and a fitted white Abercrombie T-shirt. Despite the fact that she's about ten years too old to be wearing that kind of shirt, she manages to make it work.

"Hi," I say, walking toward her. "Are you waiting on Mom?"

She shrugs, a confused look on her face. "She asked me to come over for dinner."

"Really?" I ask, surprised. "She's never home this early."

Jen frowns, twirling her keys around her index finger. "Well, I guess I can go run some errands and come back later. What time do you think she'll be here?"

"I never know," I answer honestly. "But you're welcome to come in. I was going to grill some tilapia for dinner. Sound okay?"

"Heavenly," Jen says, smiling at me with beautifully whitened teeth. "Are you sure you don't mind if I hang out until your mom gets here?"

"Not as long as you help with dinner," I say, returning her smile.

Jen pushes herself off the car and reaches out to take a bag from me. "Let me give you a hand."

"Thanks," I say, flexing my fingers to get the blood circulating again.

I unlock and open the front door, then walk to the kitchen, where I dump the grocery bags, my purse, and my backpack. I make quick work of unpacking the groceries and pulling the usual seasonings from the pantry, actually feeling comforted by Jen's unexpected presence.

"Let me just put some rice on," I say. This may not be the quiet evening I'd had planned, but it might be exactly what I need.

Jen leans against the counter, watching me work. "Do you always do the cooking?"

"Usually. Mom works so late, it's just easier if I take care of dinner."

Before I can attempt continuing the conversation, Jen begins slowly walking around the kitchen and our adjoining living room. One of my favorite things about our house is that the kitchen opens to the rest of the house, so even when I'm in the kitchen I never feel isolated. I can turn on the television and watch MTV or the Discovery Channel and be content.

Jen stops in front of a wall of pictures. Mom's added pictures to that wall over the years, and now it's nearly floor-to-ceiling framed photographs. Some are of me on various sport teams, or at school events. Some are of her at work, behind the news desk or in the field. But the majority of them are pictures of us together. My favorite picture was taken on vacation three years ago when Mom surprised me with a trip to Hawaii. We're posing at the top of Diamond Head, nothing but a stellar sunrise and beach behind us. It's particularly special since we haven't been on a vacation since then.

"Mom won't take any of them down. She just keeps adding more," I say, chopping the vegetables for a salad.

"I don't blame her," Jen says, fake news-anchor smile I can spot a mile away tossed over her shoulder. "Every single one is gorgeous."

For some reason, the word "gorgeous" sticks in my head. I've been described a million different ways, but gorgeous is not one of them.

"No pictures of your dad?" she asks quietly, scanning each frame carefully.

I shake my head. "Didn't I tell you he'd never been around?"

"Oh yeah, I guess you did mention that." She doesn't look back, just keeps staring at the pictures, like she's looking for Waldo.

I want to tell her she can keep on looking but he's not going to show up, that there never was a Daddy Dearest. But that's Mom's secret to tell, not mine.

"You don't want to have contact with him?" she asks.

I shake my head as I transfer the sliced carrots to the crystal salad bowl, growing irritated. I've seen this woman four times and we've had this particular conversation twice. Either she's digging for dirt or she's got early-onset Alzheimer's. "Not even once."

She turns from the pictures and comes back to the bar, sitting across from me. "I'm so close to my dad, I can't imagine my life without him. It makes me a little sad that you don't know yours."

"His loss," I say, doing my best to cut this dead-end conversation short.

Jen studies me for a long couple of seconds. "How did they meet? Your mom and dad, I mean. Did they go to school together?"

I finish chopping the celery, dump it into the bowl, then put the knife down. "You know, these are really better questions for my mom." In spite of the way Jen's taken to Mom and my instant liking of her, her interest in my "father" is more than a little disturbing.

"Oh, sure. I'm sorry," she says. I'm happy to see she at least has the decency to blush at the impropriety of her interrogation. "The journalist in me just insists on getting all the details."

"Occupational hazard, I guess."

She smiles, brightening her face, making her even more beautiful than I previously thought. That smile's a moneymaker. And I have a growing suspicion she knows how to use it to her advantage.

My phone vibrates on the counter and I answer it quickly. "Hey, Mom."

The familiar sounds of the newsroom can be heard behind her. "I'm leaving work. Need anything from the store?"

Drawing my eyebrows forward, I look at Jen. "No, I've already been. Jen's here."

Silence penetrates the line between us. "Hmm. Does she need me for something?"

I look at Jen before answering. She takes a swig from the bottled water in front of her, then moves away from the counter and walks aimlessly around the living room, studying the various knickknacks and journalism awards displayed on the antique bookcase.

"She said you invited her for dinner," I say quietly.

I can practically hear the wheels turning in Mom's head. "I told her she should come over *some* night, but I didn't mention tonight specifically. At least, I don't think I did."

Not knowing what to say, I stay silent and keep my eyes on Jen, wondering exactly what she's doing here.

Mom laughs, breaking my intense gaze on our guest. "Well, if she says I invited her, I'm sure I did. Sorry about the surprise. I'll be there in ten."

I close the phone and take a deep breath, a ribbon of suspicion curling its way around my spine.

Jen turns around, obviously aware my call has ended. "Was that your mom?"

"Yeah," I say, nodding. "She's on her way."

"Great," she says, smiling innocently.

✦ ✦ ✦

The following day, I set my lunch on the table in my usual spot across from Kristen and Rock.

"I've come up with a plan," Kristen says, eyes sparkling mischievously.

I sigh, looking at my lifelong best friend. "Whatever it is, it better not involve me."

"Of course it involves you. All my best plans do." She keeps her arm wrapped around Rock's as she rushes on. "I've got one word for you. Double date."

"That's two words. And no thanks."

Rock chuckles softly, eyes on mine. "I told her you'd say no. But have you ever tried to change her mind?"

"A few thousand times," I say, grinning despite the circumstances.

"Have you ever succeeded?" he asks, ignoring the daggers Kristen's shooting.

"Not even once."

"Just hear me out, Sarah," she says, slapping her hand on top of mine.

"Absolutely not. I can't think of one single thing I'd rather do less. N. O." Seriously, just the thought nauseates me. It's bad enough she's trying to set me up. I'd rather stab myself in the eye than watch Kristen and Rock paw each other all night while I force conversation with a total stranger.

"But I've already set it up."

I level my most hateful gaze on her. "Tell me you're joking."

She shakes her head. "I promise this is a good thing. It's time for you to get out and have a little fun."

I almost laugh out loud. That's exactly what I tell Mom.

"You're thinking about it," she singsongs, completely misreading my momentary silence.

"You don't want to know what I'm thinking."

Again, Rock laughs quietly. It's a low, rumbly laugh that's all testosterone and sexy as hell.

"Come on, we're doing this for you," Kristen says, retreating to full-pout mode.

"Don't include me in this craziness," Rock says.

Kristen ignores his comment. "We'll be doubling so it'll be tons of fun no matter what. You'll love it, I promise. We're going to a dramatization of *The Birthmark*. Tell me that isn't right up your alley."

I stare at her in disbelief. "You can't be serious."

Kristen folds her hands under her chin, like a child saying her bedtime prayers. "Please, Sarah. It'll be fun."

Well, at least now I know why she wants me to double with

her. There's no way she can get through *The Birthmark* and I really want to see it, but the thought of spending an evening watching Rock hang all over Kristen has me close to hyperventilating. I have to get out of this.

"Kristen," I say, imploring her with my eyes to see reason. "Look at me." I don't have to point to my nose; she understands what I'm referring to. "No one wants to date this."

"That's ridiculous." Rock scowls.

"See? Even Rock agrees," Kristen says. "I'm not taking no for an answer. It's you, me, Rock, and Jay. Friday night at seven."

"*Jay?* As in *Jay Thomas?* The one who does the Napoleon Dynamite impersonations?"

Don't get me wrong. I love a funny guy as much as anyone, but that is *so not* what this is about. And it's not like Jay isn't handsome; he is, but he's totally not my type. Not that I even knew I had a type until Rock came along. Turns out, Rock defines my type.

"Please, Sarah. Please." Kristen finally releases Rock from her grasp and grabs both my hands, like we're making some sort of fatalistic pact. And, to be honest, it kind of feels like we are.

And for everything we've been through together over the years, I hold up one finger. "One double date. One."

She walks in beauty, like the night
Of cloudless climes and starry skies;
And all that's best of dark and bright
Meet in her aspect and her eyes
—LORD BYRON

Chapter Thirteen

I consider myself pretty calm; a veritable fortress, especially when compared to most girls my age. But put me in line for a double date with Kristen and Rock and I turn into a nervous, sweaty mess.

The four of us are packed into Rock's truck—thank God it has a decent-sized backseat—and we're headed to the Arena.

I'll give Rock this, he knows where to take a girl on a date, especially for a guy so new to Houston. There aren't too many guys who would suggest a play for a date, particularly the kind of guys Kristen normally dates.

Jay and I are sitting in the backseat of Rock's truck, which gives me a bird's-eye view of Rock and Kristen holding hands across the console separating them. The space between me and Jay is considerably less intimate.

The faint scent of Rock's cologne, a scent I've come to recognize as his, penetrates my senses and makes me wish I was sitting in the front seat next to him. Anything to get closer to him. I close my eyes and breathe deeply, leaning forward just an inch to smell him even better. It's not until Jay clears his throat that I realize how insane I must look.

I'm quick to face him, doing my best to act like he didn't just catch me inhaling all the spare oxygen in the truck.

"Where're we going again?" Jay asks, focusing his attention on me, making me even more self-conscious than I already am.

"The Arena Theater. Have you been there before?" I ask.

Jay nods. "Couple of times. My dad and I like to check out the big comedy acts there. The last one we went to was Larry the Cable Guy. Talk about fun-*ny!*"

Without pause, Jay launches into a pretty impressive impersonation of the comedian, right down to the trademark "Git-r-done!" which is enough to send Kristen into a laughing frenzy.

Rock and I are relatively quiet in comparison to Kristen and Jay, letting them carry the conversation in the truck.

When Jay does a spot-on impersonation of Mr. McGinty, our peacc-loving guidance counselor, all four of us wind up laughing hysterically.

Wiping tears of laughter from my eyes, I face Jay. "You're really good."

"Seriously!" Kristen adds. "You should definitely be a stand-up."

Jay smiles at the compliment and even in the dim light of the truck, I can tell he's blushing. "Thanks."

We park in the garage, then walk to the Arena's main entrance. The four of us make a pretty nice sight, I think. Kristen and I are in sundresses, which are just the thing for the Houston heat. And the guys are both in khaki Dockers and polos. Nothing too formal, but nicer than jeans.

It's hard not to compare Jay to Rock, even though it's totally unfair to do that. I hate being compared to Kristen.

Jay is definitely no Rock, but to be honest, he's cute in an all-American, boy-next-door kind of way. He's got a real wholesome look to him. Which is about a million miles away from Rock's rugged face. Rock's more the strong, quiet type whereas Jay's definitely the life of the party.

Jay and I follow Rock and Kristen, and although we're walking side by side, we're not touching. I can't make myself look away when Rock pulls Kristen in close, like he's trying to keep her warm. Like it isn't eighty-five degrees in the steamy garage.

As we approach the entrance, Rock pauses to pull the tickets out of his wallet while Kristen and Jay debate which comedian from Blue Collar Comedy is the funniest.

Rock's humming a song that sounds familiar but I can't recall and I watch him intently, like a groupie watches her idol. When he looks up, locks eyes with me, and smiles, I nearly jump in surprise. "Ready?" he asks.

I turn to Jay, who's moved close beside me, walking in step with me. There's an easiness with Jay I can't deny. He's a comfortable guy to be around, funny and confident but not cocky.

I'm the last one to enter the theater when Jay holds open the door for us. As he releases the door, he places his hand lightly on my back, guiding me as we follow Rock and Kristen.

When his hand lingers, I can't help but feel flattered that someone as popular and nice as Jay obviously likes me. At least enough to touch me. The saying "Beggars can't be choosers" runs through my head. Almost instantly, I feel guilty for even thinking such a thing. I should be proud to be with him. I try to focus on Jay, on the feel of his hand on my back.

The theater isn't Houston's finest, but it's nice just the same. Small and intimate, which is great for this kind of event. Vendors fill the lobby, selling everything from drinks and snacks to programs and souvenirs. Even over the conflicting smells in the lobby, the scent of Rock's cologne wafts to me as I walk in his wake. I haven't noticed Jay's cologne, but I make a mental note to do find out what he smells like.

"Here we are," Rock announces, stopping at the entrance to our section. As we follow the usher to our seats, Jay keeps his hand on my back, staying so close behind me that if I stopped suddenly, he'd be on top of me. It actually feels pretty special having someone that close.

The tuxedoed usher, a college-aged guy with a barbell piercing through his right eyebrow, stands transfixed, eyes trained on my nose, when I attempt to move past him to my seat. Rock and Kristen have already shuffled down the narrow aisle and are waiting for me and Jay to follow, but I can't move out of humiliation. Which is utterly ridiculous when you consider I've dealt with this kind of thing my entire life.

But having someone gawk at me so candidly is crushing—especially on a date.

Jay gently nudges me forward as he turns to the usher, snapping his fingers millimeters from the usher's eyes. "Can I help you with something?" he asks, going from all-American funny guy to ass-kicking superhero in the blink of an eye. Maybe I can like this guy after all.

The usher steps back, mumbling something that sounds like "sorry" before hightailing it back up the aisle to man his post at the door.

I don't dare face Jay since I have absolutely no clue what to say. I can't even decide if I should say anything at all. So I totally cop out and act like nothing unusual happened. Like my date didn't have to stand up for me because I was too humiliated to do it for myself.

Not my proudest moment. Not by a mile.

I walk to my seat next to Kristen and notice her eyes are narrowed, her predictable protectiveness in action. Knowing I need to defuse her anger, I smile and wink at her to let her know I'm okay. Because if she thinks I'm truly upset, she'll go all mother-protecting-her-cub on that insignificant usher. And that wouldn't be fun for anyone.

More surprising than Jay's willingness to defend me is the way Rock's standing, watching the usher at the door. His normally placid eyes are dark and menacing, like he's doing everything he can to telepathically hurt the usher.

"Great seats, man," Jay says, jarring Rock out of his trance. Jay nods at him in an everything's-okay way and sits down.

Rock nods, reluctantly taking his seat as he lays those beautiful eyes on me. He takes a deep breath, then lets it out, and his eyes go soft again.

Looking back at Jay, Rock says, "Glad you like them."

Kristen pulls Rock's hand into hers. "I've never been here before. I love the way it's set up," she says.

Rock's eyes are back on mine as he mumbles a response. When he gives me a crooked little smile, my heart drops.

I'm spared from suffering through lame chitchat until curtain time when the lights dim, signaling the start of the play. There *is* a God.

It doesn't take long for me to forget the incident with the usher and lose myself in the play, which has a cast of only three: Georgiana, Aylmer, Aminadab.

Watching the story unfold just ten rows in front of me, I can literally feel myself on the stage as Georgiana. She's stunning with just one visible flaw: a birthmark on her cheek in the shape of a hand. And she's entirely comfortable with the birthmark. It's just a small part of who she is, like her lips or her eyes . . . or her nose. In fact, other people find it alluring.

But things change for Georgiana. Just like they've changed for me.

When her husband, Aylmer, becomes obsessed with her birthmark, insisting on its removal so she'll be flawless, she agrees in her eagerness to please him.

I flash back to the night I scanned that ridiculous Web page to check out new noses, just to make myself more attractive to Rock. More attractive to anyone, even myself.

I ache to scream out to Georgiana, "Don't do it!"

The emotions rolling through me are ludicrous. I've read the story before. I *know* she ends up dead as a result of her husband's "cure" but my stomach twists as I watch the actress take the cup of liquid from him. Tears sting my eyes and I swallow audibly. I'm too full of emotion to be embarrassed, even when Jay puts his hand on the chair behind me, letting his fingertips rub my shoulder in a soft, soothing way.

Onstage, Aminadab mutters he would never change Georgiana if she were his wife. Will someone ever feel that way about me? About my nose? I mean, a birthmark can be covered with makeup, but a nose? *My* nose? Not so much.

I swipe at the trail of tears on my face, closing my eyes to the scene being brought to life.

"Oh geez," Kristen whispers, then grabs my hand. Her death grip does little to comfort me as I open my eyes in time to see Georgiana take her last dramatic breath on stage.

Let's face it. I've had seventeen years to think about the way people see me. And how I see myself. Nine days out of ten, I'm happy to stay exactly the way I am. But on that tenth day . . . I'm not so sure I wouldn't fall for some crazy Aylmer-ish scheme to fix my nose.

✦ ✦ ✦

The other three chat without me on the ride to the restaurant because my head is still swimming with thoughts of Georgiana. A dull thud pounds in my head. I don't want to be like Georgiana, a girl so easily convinced that she has to be perfect. It's what I've preached to Kristen for years. It's what I've fought against for as long as I can remember.

I'm pulled out of my funk when we park in front of my favorite Chinese restaurant in Houston, P.F. Chang's.

When we sit at a booth near the back, Jay rests his arm behind my shoulders, leaving me frozen in place. Am I supposed to move around or sit completely still? What if his arm slips off and he thinks I'm being rude? Or worse, he thinks I'm interested? I totally play it safe and sit like I've got a motion-sensored bomb tied to my butt.

Jay doesn't seem to notice my rigidity because he laughs and cuts up over dinner, like having his arm draped over my shoulders is the most natural thing in the world. Like we do that every day.

Even when our meals come and he puts his arm down, his hand finds mine from time to time, squeezing it or brushing over it like a little reminder that he's there. And, honestly, it's totally got me flustered.

As if that wasn't enough to deal with, it's getting harder and harder to ignore the way Rock keeps looking at me. Studying me, like he's trying to read my mind. Even when Kristen attempts to pull him into her conversation with Jay, he only gives her a cursory glance, a grin, and a few words.

"What'd you think about the play?" Rock asks suddenly, interrupting Jay midsentence.

I look at Kristen, then back at Rock. "Me?"

He nods, impatient. "You."

"I've read the story before, so there weren't any surprises."

Again, he nods, growing irritated. "But the *play*? How'd it hit you?"

"It was great, Rock. Really. Thanks for the tickets." Geez. What does he expect me to say? I loved the way it tore at my gut, making me more aware of my unmistakable flaw than ever?

But he's relentless. "Do you think Georgiana was right to go along with Aylmer's plan?"

Before I can answer, Kristen pipes in, rolling her eyes. "Hel-*lo*. She ended up dead. Of course she shouldn't have gone along with it."

Rock turns his attention to his date. "That's not the point. Should she have given in to his demands to be perfect? To be what *he* wanted?" He targets me again. "Do you think she was right to do that, regardless of how it ended?"

I shake my head, fully understanding the point he's pushing. "Of course not. No one should change the way they look in order to please someone else." As the words slip through my mouth quietly, I know that's how I feel in my heart of hearts. Even on that tenth day, when I consider changing my nose, it's just that—a consideration. Curiosity. Nothing more.

The entire conversation is so intense, so confusing, my head is spinning. The table is silent and everyone's looking directly at me.

The corner of Rock's mouth turns up slightly and his eyes soften. "Is that really what you think?"

"It's really what I think," I tell him with 100 percent conviction.

✦ ✦ ✦

My hands are sweating when Rock pulls his truck to a stop in front of my house. Jay opens the door and lets me out, then walks me to the door, just like I've always imagined.

But I'm terrified.

I'm *not* ready for a kiss. Not now. Not with Jay. Especially not with Rock and Kristen watching.

"Have fun?" Jay asks, voice low, deeper than I expected.

Fun? The night was uncomfortable and emotional. But, surprisingly, it *was* fun. "I did. Thanks for going along with Kristen's double-date scheme," I whisper.

He stops suddenly, pulling me around to face him. "I've wanted to ask you out for nearly two years, but I've always chickened out. I owe Kristen."

"You do?" I ask, flattered, embarrassed.

"I'd like to do it again," he says, taking my hand as he walks me the few remaining steps that bring us to the door. "Maybe next weekend?"

"Again?" I ask, like a total idiot.

"Except maybe this time it can be just the two of us."

I nod, smiling, not entirely sure that's something I want to do. I mean, how much did the two of us actually talk tonight? Do we have anything in common? And just because he's the first guy to show some interest in me doesn't mean I *have* to go out with him. Does it?

Instead of answering him, I unlock the dead bolt. When I turn around, he's moving in.

Lower.

Closer.

He doesn't even look at my nose as he comes in for the kiss.

I'm so nervous I could puke. Right here, right now.

But then it happens. His lips graze mine, his nose bumping mine just slightly. I never even close my eyes, watching him maneuver my face with ease. When he pulls away, I stare back at him, blinking, stunned.

"See you later," he says with a run of his fingers over my hair, then turns and jogs down the sidewalk and back to the truck.

I touch my lips, wondering if it really happened.

Beauty is the promise of happiness.
—STENDHAL

Chapter Fourteen

I walk in the house as Rock's truck pulls away from the curb. The house is quiet, but there's a light on in the living room.

When I find Mom on the couch, I smile. This is how I love her best.

In cotton pajama pants and a tank top, with her hair pulled back in a messy ponytail, she looks more like my sister than my mother. She doesn't look like Beth Burke, news anchor. She's just . . . Mom.

I'm touched she attempted to wait up for me. There's an open book in her lap and a half-empty glass of wine on the table next to her, but she's sound asleep.

I slide the book out of her hand and carefully dog-ear the page to mark her spot before placing it on the coffee table. But I'm not quiet enough, because she wakes with a sleepy smile.

"What kind of mother am I?" she asks. "I can't even stay awake to make sure you get home safely."

I lie down on the couch and put my head in her lap, looking up at her face. "Don't worry about it. Neither one of us has much practice with this dating business."

She runs her hands through my hair, softly untangling it as she goes, reminding me of our earlier days together. I can't even remember the last time she touched me this way.

"Tell me all about it," she prods.

I know most girls wouldn't do it, but I'm in the mood to talk so I tell her every last detail about the night, ending with the kiss.

"What exactly were you expecting?" Mom asks.

"I don't know. Sparks? Fireworks?"

"Hate to be the one to tell you this, honey, but most kisses aren't like that."

"Don't tell me *that*," I groan.

"Sometimes, with the right man, it's amazing. I mean toe-curling, lose-your-breath intense. But, for me, those kinds of kisses have been few and far between. Way far."

"Well, there definitely wasn't any toe curling happening, that's for sure. But it wasn't awful either. Jay's a really cool guy."

Mom giggles. "Other than the kiss, how'd you like Jay?"

"He might be the funniest person I know. I mean, he can do impersonations like nobody's business."

"There are worse things than dating someone who makes you laugh."

I nod. "It's just that . . . well, I don't know. It was more like going out with a friend."

"Tell me about Rock and Kristen," she says, diverting the conversation to the real issue of the night. She's got a killer gut instinct.

"They're impossible to be around, always touching, hugging, kissing. Ugh." Even as the words leave my lips, I can hear the jealousy in my voice. I sound like a little girl who's been forced to share her toys.

"You've never had a problem with Kristen doing that with her other boyfriends," Mom says quietly, knowing she's treading on fragile ice.

"Mmm-hmm," I mumble. Kristen's list of nameless, faceless guys meant nothing . . . to either one of us.

"Maybe you should just lay it all out there. You know? Just tell her exactly how you're feeling."

"And lose the only friend I've got? No thanks. I always swore I'd never let a guy break us up. I never have and I'm not going to start now."

"I think you may be underestimating Kristen, Sarah. The two of you have been best friends practically your entire lives. Don't you think she'd understand? We both know Kristen would want you to be happy."

I roll my eyes. "I don't think so." Besides, I can't even imagine how I'd go about telling her. *Awkward.*

"What about Rock? Think you can talk to him?"

"About *him*?" Mom seriously needs to get out and date a little. Maybe then she won't come up with such outrageous ideas.

"About the *situation*," she clarifies.

"The situation is that I'm attracted to my best friend's boy-friend. There's nothing he can do to fix that." I don't let my mind think about how he was betrayed that same way or what he'd do if he found out what Kristen and I had been up to. "There's nothing I'd really *want* him to do, because in order to make me happy, he'd have to hurt Kristen, which I'm 100 percent against. And we're making a monumental assumption that he'd even consider dating me. Which, of course, he wouldn't."

Mom stops stroking my head and tweaks my nose, some-thing she used to do when I was little. When I was five, I loved it. But I've long since forbade her—or anyone else for that matter—from touching IT.

I swat at her hand. "You know I hate that."

"Lighten up, Sarah. There's so much more to you than your nose. For someone who's hell-bent on keeping her God-given nose, you sure do blame it for a lot of your problems."

I shoot up from my supine position and face her. "I do not."

"You do it every day," she says. "And, trust me, I get it. I've been there, too, remember?"

Instead of speaking, I narrow my eyes and shake my head.

"At some point, you've got to accept who you are, honey. And, believe it or not, that nose does *not* define you. That's all I'm saying."

"That's pretty big talk coming from someone who had a nose job. Not to mention the gazillion times you've tried to talk me into getting one of my own."

Mom grabs my hands, holds them tight between hers.

"Because I see you holding back, purposely making choices based on your nose and not what you really want."

My eyes burn and I blink hard to clear them. "You don't have a clue what I really want," I say, then take the stairs to my room two at a time.

✦   ✦   ✦

I'm still wide awake in bed at two in the morning, completely unable to shut down my racing mind. How could Mom even suggest that I talk to Rock about this? She is seriously deluded if she thinks I'm going to confide a shred of what I'm feeling with him.

I look at the text Kristen sent earlier in the night.

Saw that sizzling kiss. Details!

Sizzling? Is that what it had looked like from Rock's truck? I hadn't bothered replying.

My phone chirps in my hand, startling me.

No way. She can't be serious.

I pull the covers over my head, willing my phone to magically short out. But, of course, it doesn't.

It chirps again.

If I don't answer her, she'll call next and I definitely don't want to talk to her.

I stretch my arm to the nightstand, I feel around for my phone, grab it, and drag it under the covers with me. I push the trackball and see she's left me two texts, just as I thought.

Facebook. Now. BTW, what did you mean in your last
message to Rock when you wrote there were bigger things
on my face to notice than my eyes? Are you trying to tell me
something?

Every square inch of my tired body freezes in place, with
the exception of my heart, which is banging around in my
chest like the Mexican jumping beans Mom brought back
from a business trip last year. My mind races back to the message I'd typed the last time I was on Facebook. I said something
about eyes being the first thing I noticed, then . . .

Oh no.

NO!

I don't have to open the Facebook message to remember
that I'd written something about people noticing my nose
before my eyes. Damn it! I can't believe I made such a stupid
mistake. I've never actually hyperventilated, but I'm pretty
sure this is what it feels like. Shaking, I sit up and hang my
head between my legs like I've seen done on TV. As stupid as
it looks, it actually works.

It takes me a good five minutes to breathe normally and
by the time I do, I'm totally pissed. Honestly, I'm as mad at
Kristen as I am at myself. How could I let her convince me to
do this? Why did I believe we could ever get away with such a
string of lies?

Still, it was ultimately my choice to take the bait.

I have to deal with this. Now.

I shoot her back a quick text to let her know I'll check

Facebook. Turning on the lamp next to my bed, I grab the laptop from my desk and boot it up. The entire four minutes it takes my computer to come to life, I question my own sanity. I mean, I've always been the levelheaded, forward-thinking one.

I log on to Facebook and click on Kristen's in-box. Rock's profile picture grabs my attention. Maybe it's because I don't want to face his reply or my own part in this twisted lovers' triangle, but instead of clicking on the in-box, I click his picture and pull up his photo albums. The sourness in my stomach tells me I'm wrong to invade his privacy like this. He hasn't friended me on Facebook and doesn't necessarily want me dragging through his personal pictures.

Regardless, I shamelessly open the first of two albums. It's simply titled "Me."

My heart stills as I scan the photographs. The first shows Rock holding the keys to a car, I'm guessing his truck. He definitely looks a couple of years younger than he is now, but that same anything-goes smile is on his face. I click to see the next picture and it's him on a rock wall ringing the bell at the top. The other pictures are more of the same, but each one tells me something new about him. He loves trying new things, and he's always wearing that same smile, the same spark in his eyes that grabbed my attention the first time I saw him.

I open the second album titled "My Family." There are only four pictures here, but they are all so remarkable, I look through them twice. Rock and his look-alike father fishing in a boat, all suntan and smiles. Rock and his petite mother cooking in the kitchen, him holding the whisk above her head, just out of reach, and her laughing. And a picture of Rock and two girls who are equally drop-dead gorgeous. They look so much alike I think they might be twins. They all have the same eyes, so I know it has to be his sisters. How did I not know he had sisters? Does Kristen know? The last picture is of Rock and a woman who looks to be his grandmother. He towers over her small, gray head, hugging her close and smiling like he's the luckiest guy on earth.

I sit and stare at the screen, wishing I had never gotten involved with this whole Facebook mess. I mean, not only do I have to "talk" to Rock as Kristen, now I'm learning so much about him that I admire and adore that it's hard to separate what I'm writing from what I'm feeling. What the hell was I thinking when I agreed to this?

My phone chirps again.

Done yet?

I put the phone on the bed beside my laptop, knowing I'm totally screwed. If I don't write Rock back for Kristen, and she attempts to write him back herself, he'll immediately know something's going on. If I do write Rock, then I'm continuing this ridiculous scam.

But I'm in way too deep to back out now. It goes against everything inside me, but I do what I have to. I open the Facebook message from Rock and read reluctantly.

The eyes are my first attention-getter, too. Your blue
eyes were the first thing I noticed about you. There's
something about a person's eyes, isn't there? Like I can
tell you love to have fun and love to laugh; you just have
that certain mischievous spark. Take care of those
babies; they're phenomenal. I've racked my brain but I
can't figure out what you mean when you say there are
"bigger things" on your face to notice than your eyes.
There isn't one centimeter of you that isn't exactly the
way it should be. Trust me, I've studied your face enough
to know.

I stop reading and close my eyes. The thought of Rock studying Kristen's gorgeous features sends a shot of ice through my
heart. I can't imagine anyone—especially Rock—studying
my features and deciding I've reached perfection. Those kinds
of moments are exclusively reserved for the likes of Kristen. But
there's absolutely no reason to let myself go there. Then I'll just
be pissed *and* depressed. I force myself to read on.

What song makes me happy when I hear it? Great
question . . . My parents listen to a lot of R & B and jazz,
so I grew up listening to music most people don't particularly love. But one song that always makes me sing along
and smile is one I'm sure you'll know. "Can't Get Enough
of Your Love, Babe" by Barry White. Did you notice me
humming it tonight? It makes me think of you and that
always makes me happy.

165

My turn.

What would be the title of your biography?

I read the question with a smile. What better way to get down to the heart of a person? My mind circles the question. What *would* be the title of my biography? *Honker?* Umm . . . *Bigger Than Life?* And then it hits me. The title for my biography is so obvious I can't believe I didn't think of it sooner. *Some Kind of Cyrano.*

Then I remember I'm answering for Kristen. And hers comes to me easily.

True Blue. I really try to be loyal and I hope that when I'm gone, people remember me as faithful and reliable. So you pair "True" with "Blue" (for my eyes), and there you have it.

I looked through your pictures and

I stop midsentence. Maybe Kristen actually knows about the sisters. Maybe she's already talked to him about his Facebook pictures. I go back and delete the last sentence. Better play it safe. Instead I ask my next question.

I definitely want your answer to the biography question, too. So send that!

But my new question is this . . . "If you were forced to give up everything you own in exchange for one thing, what would that be?"

About that weird comment last time . . . I wrote that post right after I discovered the beginning of a zit. You know how that is . . . you're sure it's going to be the size of Everest once it erupts. But I totally whipped it into submission.

Thanks for a great night.
Love, Kristen

I quickly scan what I wrote, careful to make sure there are no traces of me in the message. So what if the excuse is pretty lame? It's the best I can do at two o'clock in the morning. If Kristen wants an answer that sounds better than that, she'll just have to write it herself.

I click Send, ready to end this farce and force myself to sleep. Maybe a plan to graciously end this disaster will come to me during the night.

Maybe.

✦ ✦ ✦

By the time I make it to the cafeteria on Monday, I've done a fine job of evading Kristen and Rock. I arrived just as journalism and lit started and was the first one out the door, eliminating any chance of chitchat. The last thing I need is a bunch of questions about how I feel about Jay.

167

But there's positively no escaping them at lunch.

"You okay?" Kristen asks when I finally make my way to our table. "You were awfully quiet this weekend."

I nod, thinking how busy I'd been Friday night being her on Facebook. "Yeah, I had a ton of homework."

"So . . . ," Kristen says with a sly smile, the very one I've been avoiding all day. "What'd you think?"

There's no way I'm making this easy for her so I totally play dumb. "About what?"

"You can't be serious," she says, rolling her eyes dramatically. "Jay, that's what."

I shrug. "He's nice. We already knew that, though, right? It's not like that was my first time to meet him."

"You know exactly what I mean, Sarah Burke. Do *not* start playing games with me."

Rock is watching me intently, setting my stomach to doing flips.

"What do you want me to say, Kristen?" I ask. "That I'm head over heels in love with him?"

"Are you?" Rock asks.

"Not hardly," I mumble. "I had fun. The play was phenomenal and you know how I feel about P.F. Chang's."

Kristen slaps her hands on the table, fed up with my vague answers. "Are y'all going out again?"

"Geez," I say, looking around to make sure no one else heard her. "Calm down, already. He asked if I wanted to go out next weekend, but I never really answered him."

"Omigod! That's awesome, Sarah!" Kristen squirms in her seat, doing her own little happy dance.

Alone.

She doesn't bother to notice that I'm not even fractionally as happy about it as she is.

"Are you going to say yes?" Rock asks, halting Kristen's celebration.

"Of course she's going to say yes," Kristen argues, then looks to me. "You *are* going to say yes, aren't you?"

I shrug again. "I don't know. I think maybe Jay and I make better friends than a couple."

"That's absurd," Kristen scoffs.

"If it's how she feels . . . ," Rock says with the smallest hint of a grin to me, like we both know the same secret.

"Before you do anything or say anything to Jay, you need to really think it through. Maybe another date is all you need to make that connection. The *love* connection." She wiggles her eyebrows in a totally ridiculous way that makes me want to laugh.

"Maybe," I concede, knowing she's wrong.

Dead wrong.

"So we'll see," she says, satisfied I haven't totally given up on Jay.

"We'll see," I lie.

+ + +

I'm not proud of it, but by eight that evening, the curiosity kills me and I shamelessly peek in on Kristen's Facebook. Just to see if he's responded to her—well, actually *my*—message. It's wrong and only serves to further torture me, but I can't stop myself. I'm definitely on what Mom would call a "slippery slope."

I look through her home page and see the usual people and quizzes filling the screen, save one. I'm simultaneously satisfied and disappointed when I see Rock hasn't replied. I log out of Kristen's Facebook account and log in to mine. It's noticeably less busy than Kristen's but I do have something she doesn't.

A message.

Okay, it's not really a *message*. But it's something. It's a friend request. From Rock.

Despite the fact it took him so long to friend me, I click Confirm.

To further torment myself, I sit and wait, thinking maybe . . . just maybe . . . he'll be waiting for me to reply like he was when Kristen confirmed him.

Knowing I can't very well sit in front of the computer until—and IF—he sends me a message, I leave the laptop and busy myself by picking up Ringo's toys off the floor and dropping them into the little white basket sitting on the hanging swing.

I open my phone, check to make sure the ringer's on and that I haven't missed any messages from Mom or Kristen, then put it back on the nightstand.

After what seems like an eternity, I go back to my laptop and refresh my Facebook page to see if there are any new messages. I don't know what I expect him to say other than "Hi" and "Thanks for sharing your scorching-hot BFF with me."

But I check it anyway.

And there's nothing.

Not even so much as a "Thanks for friending me."

What did I expect? It's exactly what I deserve.

+ + +

Later that week, I walk into Jacobi's room seconds before the bell rings, something he thoroughly disapproves of. When I give him a quick apologetic smile, he scowls, leaving me to shuffle off to my desk like a scolded dog.

Rock gives me a small grin before I drop into my seat. "Cutting it close, aren't you?"

I nod, knowing I don't have a decent answer. I mean, it's not like I can just come right out and say "Well, you know, I'm totally avoiding you because I'm shamelessly in love with you."

Jacobi saves me from humiliating myself with his booming voice. "You should have read chapters ten through thirteen last night. Does anyone have a question or a comment about what you read?"

Normally, I'd throw out a comment, but I'm not exactly at the top of my game these days.

The room remains silent, no one willing to be first to step out and offer their thoughts. Thankfully, Jacobi doesn't push it—like he so often does—and moves on.

"Well, then, this assignment should be a snap. Let's begin by returning to our partners from last week. This week you'll be dissecting a quote from the novel and comparing it to real-life situations. You are expected to show me exactly how that quote applies to your life today. Right here in these halls, or at home, or at work. I assure you every single quote I'm assigning has modern-day applications. So no excuses."

I turn my desk around so that it's face-to-face with Rock's. Despite the effort I've put into ignoring him all day, I can't stop myself from smiling. Just seeing his face makes me happy. Stupid, stupid, stupid.

Jacobi drops the quote on the desk in front of me.

"Want me to read it aloud?" I ask.

Rock nods. "Go for it."

I pull the paper closer to me and read our assigned quote from *The Scarlet Letter*.

"Let men tremble to win the hand of woman, unless they win along with it the utmost passion of her heart! Else it may be their miserable fortune . . . when some mightier touch than their own may have awakened all her sensibilities, to be reproached even for the calm content, the marble image of happiness, which they will have imposed upon her as the warm reality."

When I finish reading, I look up to find Rock's eyes on mine.

Nervous and unsure of what to say, I start rambling. "It's a biggie this time, that's for sure. I mean, it sounds pretty easy to understand, we just need to figure out how we can apply it to real life today. I mean, not *today* today, but 'today.'" I end with the finger quotes when I say the last "today," making me inwardly cringe. I seriously hate myself.

Instead of laughing at me, Rock puts his hand on mine, setting off a series of firecrackers in my chest. Now *this* is the kind of spark I was talking about.

"Let's just start with the quote," he says, then abruptly removes his hand. The warmth falls away with his hand, but the electricity continues to jump beneath my skin. "Can you read the first sentence again?"

I quickly put my eyes back on the paper and read the sentence, willing myself to read slowly, like a *sane* person. "Let men tremble to win the hand of woman, unless they win along with it the utmost passion of her heart!"

Rock clears his throat before speaking. "He's saying you shouldn't want the hand of a woman—marriage—unless you have her passion as well. I guess that really applied to the era Hawthorne was writing about. These days, most people only marry because they want to. At least in America, arranged marriages are a thing of the past."

I nod, but then stop. "I think I see how it can apply today, though. I mean, don't you think people get married for the wrong reasons, without the passion Hawthorne's talking about? Think of all the people that marry for money, or stature, or because they got pregnant, and then leave that spouse for someone else. Someone with the 'mightier touch.'"

"Good point," Rock says, his crooked smile knocking my socks off. I'm literally expecting my shoes to just fly right off my feet and club Jacobi in the head. "What about the next sentence?"

"Else it may be their miserable fortune . . . when some mightier touch than their own may have awakened all her sensibilities, to be reproached even for the calm content, the marble image of happiness, which they will have imposed upon her as the warm reality."

"Okay," Rock begins. "So he's saying that if you marry someone without passion you'll be miserable."

"Right," I agree. "And when you realize you've kept that person from being with someone they truly feel passionate about, you'll have to answer for that."

Rock nods, brow furrowed. "What about the marble image of happiness?"

"It's fake. She looks happy on the outside, but it's just an image. It's not real."

"I've never thought of that before. You?" Rock asks.

"I don't know. I guess I think about what it'd be like to be with the wrong person," I say, then instantly wish I could rewind time and take it all back.

"Like with Jay?" he asks, serious eyes penetrating me.

I shrug in answer. "Jay's a nice guy. But passion?"

"Not so much?" Rock asks, his eyes deep and intense, like they'd been at P.F. Chang's.

"Well, I'm not exactly an expert, but I'd have to say no."

Rock smiles just enough to reveal his endearing teeth. "Kristen would kill me if she knew I was saying this, but I told her he wasn't a match for you. You need someone more . . . I don't know."

More like you, I think.

But instead he says, "More cerebral."

"*Cerebral*?" I ask, shocked at his word choice. "Am I that big of a nerd?"

He laughs. "No, Sarah. I just think you'd get bored with someone who's biggest contribution to a conversation is an impersonation. Regardless of how good it is."

174

"He *is* good, though, isn't he?"

Rock nods, then puts his hand back on mine, freezing any logical thought I was trying to form. "The right guy's out there, you know. I'm sure of it."

"Right," I say, simultaneously wishing he'd move his hand and keep it there. Talk about heaven and hell.

"You don't believe me?" he asks.

I pull my hand away and place it back in my lap to stop myself from climbing over the desk and kissing him. "What if you find the right person but it's not the right time?" I ask.

Rock rests his chin on his folded hands. "Give me an example."

An example? How am I supposed to come up with a good example without totally incriminating myself?

"Come on, you have to have a situation in mind," he says.

And that look in his face, that genuine concern and total openness has me thinking I should just say it. I mean, just come right out and say it. *Rock, it's you.*

I hear Mom's voice in my head urging me. *Just spit it out it, Sarah.*

"Rock . . ." I pause, never taking my eyes off his because then I'll totally lose my nerve. Eye to eye like this, it just feels right. It's the right time to tell him. "It's—"

"Time's up!" Jacobi announces, and the shuffle of desks, chairs, and students drowns out the final word "you" as it falls from my mouth.

Rock looks at me, confused. "What? I didn't hear you."

I shake my head, realizing how close I'd come to ruining the most important relationship in my life. What was I thinking? Okay, well, I wasn't thinking. Not about Kristen, anyway. I was drowning in Hawthorne's words and Rock's eyes.

"Nothing. It was nothing," I say, grabbing my books and bolting from the room.

Damn Hawthorne.

Beauty is the gift of God.
—ARISTOTLE

Chapter Fifteen

When I walk into the library for study hall, Kristen's already there, sitting on the edge of her chair, looking around the room anxiously. I seriously consider bailing and hiding out in the restroom for the next forty-five minutes since I'm still reeling from nearly spilling my guts to Rock. But I know it's just my guilty conscience and that's not Kristen's fault.

She spots me and waves furiously, like I could possibly miss her. She's practically standing in her seat and screaming my name to get my attention.

I nod, hoping she'll sit down before we get in trouble. Of course, she doesn't. She just keeps on bouncing up and down until I get there. She looks like she's about to burst. It takes all my self-control to not laugh out loud. Kristen can make me laugh like no one else.

"Too much Red Bull, I see," I say, taking my usual seat.

"You *have* to read Rock's letter." She tosses a folded piece of paper across the table to me, and I swear, even the paper's happy the way it skitters toward me.

"Read it!" she orders.

There is nothing—absolutely nothing—I want to do less.

Flicking the paper back to her, I shake my head. "That's between you and Rock. I'm done."

"What?" she asks, shock evident in her huge blue eyes. "When did you stop caring about my love life?"

Umm . . . roughly since you started dating Rock.

"Give me a break," I say. "I think I've shown more than enough interest. Especially when it comes to these letters, and let's not even get started on the whole Facebook farce."

"So why stop now? I'm just asking you to read it." She unfolds the paper and looks at me.

I close my eyes, attempting to transport my mind to someplace else. Anywhere else.

She starts reading it aloud, her voice a library-appropriate whisper, for once. "Just when I think I've figured you out, you surprise me. For someone to be so stunning and so bright is rare, and I consider myself the luckiest guy in Texas to have found you. Every second counts when I'm with you."

When she stops reading, I slowly open my eyes, praying they don't reveal the pain slicing through me. Because those words should be mine. It may be her eyes, her face, her hair he dreams of, but the words he's fallen in love with are 100 percent mine.

"Well?" she asks. "Don't you think that's just about the sweetest thing you've ever heard?"

I chew my bottom lip before answering, afraid the entirely wrong thing will slip out. "It's something, all right."

"We have to answer him. I can't just leave it at that. But I don't have a clue where to start. What do you think about—" She stops talking when she notices me shaking my head.

"Forget it, Kristen."

"You can't abandon me now. He'll know!" Her voice creeps past a whisper and threatens to grow into full-blown hysteria.

"At some point, you're going to have to do this on your own. Do you seriously expect me to keep doing things like this for you?"

"Actually, I do. It's what friends do for each other."

"You know I love you like a sister, Kris. Your happiness means the world to me. But I can't keep writing letters to Rock. It's getting creepy. Besides, he already likes you. I think you're safe to be yourself."

"Are you *crazy*? Do you have any idea where he wants to go this weekend? A poetry reading at some chocolate bar in artsy-fartsy Montrose. A *poetry reading*, Sarah! What in the world do I know about poetry?"

"Why don't you suggest doing something else? Something you'd both enjoy?"

"Right," she scoffs. "I'm sure a stroll through the mall is exactly what Rock has in mind for a romantic evening."

"I don't know what to tell you, Kristen. Just respond to his comments. And listen to what they're reading. You might actually enjoy it."

The thought of Kristen at a poetry reading with Rock

makes me want to laugh and cry at the same time because I wish it were me. *I'm* the one who loves poetry. And a reading at a chocolate bar? That's got to be the sexiest date ever.

Poetry + Chocolate + Rock = HEAVEN!

"I can't even concentrate on that right now. My mind is totally fixated on writing him back. If I don't answer him, he'll think I've lost interest."

"Then you really ought to write him."

"Not *me*. You." She points her finger at me, obviously frustrated I won't give in.

"I'm sorry, Kris. I just . . . can't. Please understand." I look her in the eye, hoping she'll see how much she means to me and how much it hurts me to tell her no.

"I can't believe this," she says, shock and hurt etched in her face. She doesn't bother folding the paper, just shoves it into her messy binder and storms away.

✦ ✦ ✦

It's not until I'm driving home alone after school that the full impact of my argument with Kristen hits me. Even though I did something I knew was wrong to help her, I've still lost her. But I can't keep writing Rock for her, especially when every word I write expresses how I feel. Isn't that more deceitful than *not* writing the letters for her?

I drive to the house and park in the garage, then pull the key from the ignition.

No one's home.

And no one's going to be home for hours.

This is not the night for me to sit around and think. Tonight, thinking could be dangerous. I'm dying to read Rock's reply. But I decide I've got to go cold turkey and just end it. No turning back.

Shoving the keys into the ignition, I back out of the driveway and head to the station, my home away from home. And since I still need to get the scholarship application from Jen, I actually have a reason to go.

When I walk through the double glass doors, it's ten minutes to six. I have just enough time to grab the application before surprising Mom on the set.

I weave my way through the newsroom, waving to familiar faces. Jen's not in her cubicle, so I search her desk for a sticky note to let her know I came by for the application.

"I think she's in Vic's office," an unfamiliar voice says through the cubicle wall.

"Thanks," I say, tossing the sticky note in the trash before walking in the direction of the producer's office, which is right next to Mom's. If Jen's not finished meeting with Vic, she will be soon because Vic has to be on the set in five short minutes.

When I get to Mom's office, I drop my keys on her credenza, then wait in the hallway for Jen. Through the half-open door to Vic's office, I can hear Jen talking quietly, which, from what I know about her, isn't her norm.

Even though I know it's rude, I strain my ears to hear what she's saying. But it's Vic's voice I hear first.

"That's the most ludicrous thing I've ever heard," Vic says. "You're barking up the wrong tree on this one."

Jen sighs. "I'm telling you, Vic. I'm right about this."

"You expect me to believe that Beth Burke, Houston's top news anchor, is a lesbian?"

Mom?

Lesbian?

It takes everything in me not to burst through Vic's door and slap that little backstabbing prima donna right across her Botoxed face. Because my mom has some secrets—we all do— but being lesbian isn't one of them. And if she was, she'd be proud of the fact. She'd never cower from the truth. It's what she values above everything else.

"I'm just trying to save the station some embarrassment."

Vic's chair squeaks under his weight. "I've known Beth over ten years. I've known you six weeks. Why should I believe you?"

"Why would I lie?" she asks, voice sounding about as ferocious as a newborn kitten.

"I can think of a couple of reasons," Vic says, and I nearly jump in the air and shout "Go Vic!"

Like Vic, I can think of a handful of reasons why Jen would undermine my mother, not the least of which is her desire to get to the top. No matter who she leaves in pieces behind her.

"Just think about it," Jen says. "That's all I'm asking. If our viewers think she's been hiding something like this, it will destroy their trust in her. Loss of trust translates to a loss of ratings. Ratings you've worked a lifetime to build. I care too much about this station, about you, to see that happen."

Oh. My. God.

Now she's totally kissing Vic's ass, which is so . . . eww! But knowing she's thrown Mom under the bus to get what she wants has my blood on fire. I can literally feel veins popping in my neck.

The sound of chairs moving tells me they're coming to the door, so I jump into Mom's office, where I'm out of sight but still have a view of the hallway where they're standing.

"I've got a newscast to run," Vic says, walking away from Jen like a man running from Lucifer himself. Or *her*self, as the case might be. Maybe he's a smarter man than I give him credit for being.

Jen swings the door open to Mom's office, totally catching me by surprise. But it's evident she's even more shocked than I am, judging from the look of alarm on her face. It's an expression I find tremendously satisfying.

Squirm, baby, squirm.

"What are you doing here? Your mom didn't say you were coming by today." Jen holds her dainty hand over her chest, no doubt trying to keep her heart from leaping right out of her Ann Taylor cardigan (which, now that I think about it, looks a lot like the kind of outfit Mom would wear).

"She didn't know," I say. "I actually came by to get the application from you, but you're obviously busy, so I'll catch up with you after the broadcast."

When I stand and walk around her, she doesn't move, but I can feel her eyes on my back until I enter the studio.

✦　✦　✦

I watch the broadcast through a red haze. The more I replay Jen's words in my head, the madder I get. If that little snake thinks she can ramrod my mother's career into the ground she's in for a very rude awakening.

I spend the entire broadcast aching to tell Mom what I heard, but knowing how hurt she'll be. She actually thought she had a friend in Jen. Hell, *I* thought she had a friend in Jen.

Mom didn't realize how right she was when she said good friends you can trust are hard to find. Yes, she can be a total pain in the butt and sometimes self-absorbed, but Kristen is the real thing. She's the kind of friend you fight to keep, no matter how long it takes. Kristen and I both have some work to do on our friendship if we don't want it to go down in flames.

I decide to wait until we get home before saying anything to Mom. That way we can scream, get mad, and plot revenge in private. Not that Mom would ever exact revenge on a well-deserving witch like Jen. She's too good for that.

I, on the other hand, wouldn't think twice about it.

"Meet me in my office," Mom says at the end of the broadcast, taking off her microphone and opening her cell phone. "We'll go to dinner."

Nodding, I smile at her, so proud of who she is and what she's accomplished. Seeing her in action only fuels my fury toward Jen.

When I get to Mom's office, Jen is sitting on one of the oversized chairs inside.

"I got that application for you," Jen says, pointing to a

packet of papers on the table, like she isn't the biggest liar on the planet.

I can't force myself to answer.

"Are you okay?" Jen asks me innocently. "You seem upset."

To say I'm upset would be like saying Antarctica is a little cool in the winter. And just looking at her all cozied up in Mom's office, like it's *her* office . . . honestly, it's more than I can stand.

"I wouldn't get too comfortable," I say quietly. Instead of sitting near Jen, because God knows I don't trust myself, I lean against Mom's desk, arms folded across my chest.

Jen's once-angelic face has taken on an entirely different appearance. The edge of her jaw is sharper, her nose more pointed. Even her eyes seem dark and cold. How could I have missed this Jen? The *real* Jen?

"What do you mean, Sarah?" she asks.

"I heard what you told Vic." My voice shakes, my eyes burn. But I'll be damned if I let her see me cry. Burkes don't cry in public, especially in front of their enemies. Mom's got very definite opinions about that.

"What do you *think* you heard?" she asks, unfolding her legs and leaning forward, doing her best to intimidate me.

"I *know* what I heard. And I'm telling Mom everything the second we leave this building."

Jen taps her fake fingernails together. "That would be a mistake," she says, an evil grin on her face that sends a chill down my spine.

But I'm too pissed to let it stop me.

"Let me tell you about mistakes, Jen Masters," I say, my voice finally steady and strong. Maybe I've got more of Mom in me than I realize. She'd be proud. "Mom's mistake was ever letting you into her life. She's eons ahead of you in every way that matters: beauty, intelligence, and class." I hold up a finger for each word; of course, my hands are shaking, so the move loses some of its impact.

Jen's eyes shoot to the door. Geez, she's such a scaredy-cat. "Sarah . . . ," she says.

"You'll do yourself a favor by just sitting and listening for a change. *My* mistake was trusting you to be friends with my mother. I should have known when you came over unannounced that you were scrounging for dirt."

Again, Jen looks at the door, no doubt waiting on my mother to pop in. But I completely ignore her and storm on. "And *your* mistakes? Your mistakes are so vast I can't even begin to list them. But your biggest by far was lying about my mother to make yourself look better." A sarcastic laugh slips through my lips. "And you thought *Vic* would believe you? They've been working together for years. They trust each other. She'd have no reason to hide anything from him—or her viewers for that matter."

"That's enough," a voice says, calm and strong.

But it's not Jen's voice.

It's Mom's.

I spin on my heel so fast I make myself dizzy, but I quickly recover and walk to Mom's side. Reaching for her hand, I squeeze my love and strength into her, unsure of how much she's heard.

"What's going on?" she asks slowly, like she really doesn't want to know the answer.

Jen jumps from her seat and walks toward us. "It's just a misunderstanding," she says, dismissing me with a wave of her dainty hands. "You know how kids can misinterpret what they hear."

"That may be true for some kids," Mom says, her voice steady and level. She's in emotionless-news-anchor mode. "But I can promise that's not true for Sarah. She's got better instincts about people than I ever had."

"Don't be so sure," I say.

"What did you hear, Sarah?" Mom asks, her eyes still locked on Jen.

"She told Vic lies about you."

"What kind of lies?" Mom asks.

"She told Vic you're a lesbian." I say it quietly, hoping the softer I say the words, the softer the blow. But there's no escaping the pain of a knife being shoved in your back.

Mom doesn't react like you'd expect someone to, full of hatred and vengeance. For a second, I think maybe she didn't hear me. But when she finally speaks to Jen, it's clear she has.

"I trusted you and helped you. More than once, I've gone to bat for you when Vic wanted to pull your story. But what hurts the most is that I let you into our lives, which were pretty darn great without you. Just like they'll be when you're gone."

"Beth," Jen says, her eyes pleading.

"You've lied to further your own agenda, friendship be damned."

"You don't understand." Jen's face has gone from devious to destroyed.

Mom moves closer to Jen, releasing my hand. "Don't ever come near me or my daughter again. I'll expect a written and signed admission of the lie you told on both mine and Vic's desks in the morning. Otherwise, I'll lodge a complaint against you so scathing that the only job you'll get at a news station is delivering coffee to real journalists. Like me."

Piercing daggers shoot from Jen's eyes as she pushes past us and out the door.

Mom heaves a huge sigh. "Well."

"Are you okay?" I ask, hugging Mom so tightly I think I've popped her back.

She laughs. "I'm okay if you're okay."

"Then we're good," I say.

"No," Mom says. "We're better than good. The two of us together? We're fabulous."

That which is striking and beautiful is not always good,
but that which is good is always beautiful.
—NINON DE L'ENCLOS

Chapter Sixteen

The urgency pulsing through me to make things right with Kristen is even stronger after witnessing everything Jen put Mom through tonight. When I tell Mom I need to go to Kristen's house, she doesn't ask questions.

I fly down the familiar subdivision streets and stop with a screech in front of her house. I knock, then unlock and open the door the same way I've entered her house for as long as I can remember.

Kristen's sitting on the couch, bowl of popcorn in her lap, TV on. She doesn't say anything, but she doesn't kick me out, either.

A good sign, I guess.

Now that I'm here, I'm not sure how to fix things. Especially since I've already decided I won't write the letters or Facebook messages anymore.

"Can I sit down?" I ask, which sounds so formal, so wrong.

"Suit yourself," she says, muting the television but avoiding my eyes.

I sit cross-legged on the couch and face her. "I'm sorry about this afternoon. You've been the absolute best friend ever and I didn't mean to hurt your feelings or make you mad."

Kristen smirks with a sideways glance. "Yeah, I really wasn't expecting you to say no. You don't do that a lot."

Nodding, I smile back. "I've spoiled you."

"You're telling me," she says with a giggle. "Honestly, after I thought about what you said, it made sense. I mean, I guess it *is* kind of weird to have you keep writing to Rock. You're just so good at it. Whatever I write sounds so second grade in comparison."

"You don't give yourself enough credit." I'm so happy she sees my point of view I could hug her. Standing my ground with Kristen is definitely new territory for me.

"Does this mean I have to stick up for myself now?" I ask, half joking but seriously hoping she'll still be there for me.

"You've always been able to do that for yourself, but I like doing it. Gives me an outlet for all my frustration."

I laugh out loud, knowing how true that statement is. I swear, she enjoys the verbal barbs with my tormenters way too much.

"Are we okay?" I ask tentatively.

"You know I can't stay mad at you."

"Good, because you won't believe what happened tonight,"

I say, grabbing a handful of popcorn before diving headfirst into the drama at the station.

✦ ✦ ✦

When I walk into the cafeteria the following day, Rock and Kristen are already seated. Directly across from Kristen is someone who looks suspiciously like Jay Thomas. Same neatly styled blond hair, same lean build. When the three of them burst out laughing, I'm positive it's Jay. Only he can make Kristen laugh that hard.

After zipping through the line, I drop my salad on the table and sit across from Rock, whose eyes are soft and warm, just like everything thing else about him. The sad thing is I really miss our Facebook messages. I'd begun looking forward to reading them and seeing what question he'd come up with next.

Aside from his annoying habit of dating my best friend, I really and truly think I might love him. Not in the typical high-school-crush way, either. I mean the real thing.

"Hi, Sarah," Jay says, wadding up the paper wrapper his burger came in. I swear, guys eat entirely too quickly. It's so unhealthy.

"Hi," I answer, then turn my focus to Rock and Kristen. "Sorry I'm late. I had to grab a scholarship application from the office."

"Another one?" Kristen grumbles sympathetically. "How many of those things have you filled out?"

"All the ones I qualify for," I tell her truthfully. It's not that

Mom hasn't saved for college, because she has. But I think it's my duty to help out as much as possible. I mean, college is expensive, and I'd love it if Mom could keep some of the college savings for herself. She's way overdue some serious spa time.

"We were just talking," Kristen says, giving me a cautious look coupled with a mischievous grin.

"About?" I ask, keeping my eyes on my best friend. When she glances at Jay, I know exactly where this is headed.

"Apparently," Jay says, taking over the conversation, "these two are headed down to Montrose for some poetry and chocolate and they want us to come along."

Oh no, no, no. I am *so* not doubling with Kristen and Rock. Not again.

"This weekend might be bad," I say, shaking my head as I run through every possible excuse in my head, but it's not like I've got a bunch of excuses on standby. Guys haven't exactly been knocking my door down.

"The whole weekend?" Jay asks, brows drawn down in skepticism. I'll give him this much: at least he's smart enough to realize I'm floundering.

"Maybe," I say. "Mom and I talked about going on a weekend shopping trip to Salado." Which isn't a total lie. We did talk about going to Salado, a small Texas town known for its antique shops and art museums.

Once.

A couple of months ago.

"Really?" Kristen asks, shocked at the news. She knows better than anyone that Mom and I don't get away much.

"Maybe," I say, avoiding Kristen's eyes.

"Why didn't you say something last night?" she asks, totally not letting me off the hook.

"Well, you know, we were talking about other things. I guess I forgot."

Kristen is absolutely not buying the load of crap I'm trying to dish out. In fact, I'm pretty sure no one at the table is convinced. But I shoot her a "save me" look and, like the best friend she's always been, she digs me out of the hole I'm in.

"That's too bad," she says, dragging a french fry through the lake of ketchup on her plate. "Could've been fun."

"Tell you what," Jay says, reaching into his back pocket and pulling out his cell phone. "Give me your cell and I'll check with you this weekend. Maybe your plans will change."

"Oh yeah. Um, sure," I stammer, then quickly spout out my cell number.

"Let me see your cell phone," Jay says, hand extended. "I'll put my number in yours so you can reach me."

Like an obedient child, I pull the phone out of my purse and hand it over, then watch as he programs his information.

"I'd better run," Jay says, jumping backward out of his seat. "I've got some homework I need to catch up on before next period."

Rock nods his head. "See you around, Jay."

"Sure thing. Talk to you later, Sarah," Jay says, then walks away from our table and out of the cafeteria.

"What was *that* all about?" I ask, directing my question

solely at Kristen. Rock knows I'm not interested in Jay, so I'm positive another double date wasn't his big idea.

Kristen shrugs. "I just think you're really missing the boat with that guy. You *did* have fun last weekend, right?"

"That's not the issue here, Kristen. You can't keep setting me up like this. I actually have an opinion about who I want to date. Or *not* date, as the case may be."

"I just don't get it," she says. "You're not marrying the guy, just getting out of the house and kicking up your heels a little. It's our senior year, Sarah. It's okay to have a little fun."

There's no arguing with Kristen. I've known it for years but for some reason, I still try. I look to Rock for support, but he's got the good sense to keep his mouth closed, watching the two of us intently.

"Don't look at me," he says with a grin. "No way am I getting involved in this."

Huffing out an exasperated breath, I look at my two favorite people sitting across from me. "Look, just . . . don't do me any favors, okay? I can take care of my social life on my own. I appreciate the invitation to join you this weekend, but I'm not going. Not alone, not with Jay, not with anyone else. Okay?"

Kristen nods, her eyes apologetic. "Okay, Sarah. Whatever you say."

✦　✦　✦

Jay is waiting for me when I make it to my car after school. Leaning against the hard black steel makes him look even paler, but still good looking. Just not for me. Actually, the more I see him and Kristen together, the more I think they should be dating. But I guess that's just wishful thinking.

I smile at him as I get closer. "Are you stalking me?" I tease.

"Guilty." He pushes off the car when I unlock it and opens the door for me.

"What's up?" I ask, knowing deep in my gut exactly what he's doing at my car and wishing I had some graceful way to let him down.

"I know you said you were going out of town this weekend, but I thought maybe you'd change your mind if you knew the date would be solo. You know, just the two of us. Unless you think we still need chaperones," he says with a cute little wink. And for the first time, I notice he's got dimples.

"I don't think it's going to work out for this weekend," I say, tossing my backpack onto the passenger seat. I stand in the open doorway of my car and face Jay. "Mom's really looking forward to this trip."

Even as I say it, I think I just might be going to hell for all the lies I'm telling this lovable guy who's done absolutely nothing wrong.

"Sure, I understand," he says, a knowing look in his eyes. "Maybe next week we can grab some dinner or a movie on the weekend."

Okay, so my plan of letting him down easy and watching him ride off into the sunset isn't going to fly. It's time for me to put on my big-girl panties and deal.

"It's just that my plate is really full right now. I've got a ton of scholarship applications to complete and homework that never ends."

Jay nods. "Me, too. In fact, I'm pretty sure all the seniors are dealing with the same things. But . . ."

He stops, looking at me closely. Not at my nose, but directly into my eyes, like he's willing me to read his mind.

"What?" I whisper.

"You know, Sarah, I really like you. I think you're one of the smartest, prettiest girls at Northwest. I hope you'll give me another shot sometime. It's kind of hard to connect on a date when you're doubling, you know?" The unspoken part of his message is clear: it's hard to connect on a double date with Rock. Maybe Jay was astute enough to figure that out. It's becoming clear there's a lot more to Jay than the clown I've always pegged him to be.

I nod, keeping my thoughts to myself, wishing this awkward conversation would just end already.

Jay looks down at his feet. "Can I tell you something? As a friend?"

I cringe. That's never a good setup. "Sure."

"I've watched you a lot over the years—"

"You have?" I ask, interrupting in spite of myself. "When?"

He laughs. "That's beside the point, Sarah."

"To you, maybe. But to me, it's news." Someone's been watching me and I didn't notice? How is that even possible?

"Do you realize how many people look at you at school? How many people say hi to you in the hallway that you completely ignore?" he asks.

I shake my head. "The only things I hear in the hallway are snide remarks. And, trust me, I'm well aware of all the gawking at my nose. I'm not blind."

"I wouldn't be so sure about that. Do you even realize I'm the one who's bought you the pink carnations every year at Valentine's?"

"The ones left in my locker?" I ask, stunned. "Kristen and I have exchanged carnations for years. I just assumed they were all from her."

"Afraid not."

I stare at Jay, wondering how I could have missed that—missed him—all these years. Before Rock came along, Jay might have been someone I'd been interested in. He could've been the one taking me to school every day or the one who stayed up late at night planning the perfect date for us. And I've cheated myself out of that for years and didn't even know it.

"You know, when we went out last weekend, you never took your eyes off Rock."

"I—"

"It's okay," he says, holding up his hands to stop me. "I'm cool with that. I know you'd never hurt Kristen by betraying her that way. Honestly, I'd still like you to give me another shot."

"I don't know," I say, shell-shocked. Part of me wonders why he'd even bother with me if he knows I'm into Rock. The other part of me wonders how I've missed Jay watching me for years. I mean, it would have been nice to know he was interested.

"I've been trying to figure you out for years, Sarah. I've finally gathered enough courage to ask you out, and you won't even give me a chance. What does that say about you?"

His words swim through my head.

Looking at him, I shake my head, then drop into the seat of my car. "You're a nice guy, Jay. But you don't have a clue what you're talking about."

Jay shoves his hands in his pockets. "Think about it, Sarah. Just think about it."

I slam the car door shut and start the engine without saying good-bye.

Then I watch Jay walk to his car, shoulders hunched, eyes on his feet.

And I can't shake the feeling in the pit of my stomach where his words have landed.

Could he actually be right about me?

The best part of beauty is that which
no picture can express.
—SIR FRANCIS BACON

Chapter Seventeen

Instead of heading home to obsess over Jay's parting words, I run through Sonic for the biggest Cherry Vanilla Dr Pepper they sell, then head for Kristen's house. Rock's truck is parked in the driveway, but it doesn't stop me from jogging up the sidewalk. I realize, of course, that being around Rock is probably not in my best mental interest, but I have to talk to Kristen about Jay.

I pause at the door, stopping myself from barging in like normal. I definitely don't want to witness those two half-dressed on the living room floor. Instead, I ring the doorbell and wait.

When the door swings open, it's Rock on the other side, looking like an honest-to-God, sexy-as-hell dream come true.

"Hey, you!" he says, obviously surprised to see me. "Come on in."

Against my better judgment, I follow him inside, wondering where Kristen is.

He walks toward the kitchen, totally at home. I guess I should have realized Rock was spending a lot of time at Kristen's house, but I'd never let my mind go there. There's no denying it now. A shot of pure, torturous envy races through me; my heartbeat thumps in my ears.

"Kristen's just whipping up something for us to snack on," he says, entering the kitchen. The words flow from his mouth like it's the most natural thing on earth for Kristen to cook. But I know what a disaster she is in the kitchen.

I stop short when I see her cramming a huge wad of bread into the toaster, plastic cheese wrappers strewn across the counter. She glances at me over her shoulder, a look of horror in her eyes.

"Hey," I say slowly, trying to figure out how to salvage her snack without totally outing her. "Need some help?"

She nods, then returns her attention to the abused toaster.

I face Rock with an apologetic smile, desperate to get him out of the kitchen. "Would you mind getting my backpack out of the car for me? I totally forgot it."

"Sure thing," he says, shooting me a breath-stopping wink and sending my heart straight into my throat.

As soon as he's out of the house, I unplug the toaster and dig out the bread. "Why in God's name are you massacring this defenseless bread?"

"He was hungry," she says, like that explains the two slices of Texas toast and slab of cheese she'd been forcing into the toaster.

"So you thought you'd burn the house down?"

"I was trying to make him a grilled cheese," she whines, dropping onto the stool in defeat. "This is exhausting."

"It's okay," I say, tossing the mess into the trash. "I'll take over. Just relax."

Kristen grabs my Sonic cup and takes a swallow. "Heaven in a cup," she says, taking several more deep draws on the straw.

Knowing Kristen's kitchen almost as well as my own, I grab a skillet from the cabinet, the loaf of Texas toast from the pantry, and butter and cheese from the fridge.

The door slams closed, but Kristen doesn't look up. She keeps her lips on the straw and sucks the drink in big gulps. "Here you go," Rock says, putting my nearly empty backpack on the counter.

"Thanks," I answer, keeping my eyes on the food in front of me.

"You taking over kitchen duty?" Rock asks me.

"What can I say? Cooking's my passion."

"Why'd you come over? Everything okay?" Kristen asks, getting herself back into the conversation.

"Do I need a reason?" I reply, eyes still on the skillet, my back to Kristen and Rock.

"You don't *need* a reason, but you almost always have one."

I nod. "Something really weird happened after school today."

"What?" Kristen asks.

"Jay was waiting for me by my car."

Rock lets out a little half grunt. "Why would he do *that*?"

"Hel-*lo*," Kristen sings. "He's totally hot for Sarah. Can't you tell by the way he looks at her? I swear, Sarah, that boy's got it bad for you."

"After the brush-off you gave him at lunch, I'm surprised he had the guts to face you again," Rock says, eyes narrowed.

"That's what I was hoping," I say, redirecting my attention to the skillet to flip the trio of grilled sandwiches.

"I swear, as long as I live, I will never understand you," Kristen says, shaking her head like a disappointed teacher. "You don't know a good thing when you've got it."

Without answering, I slide the spatula under the buttery sandwiches and place them on a bright blue platter. I cut them into quarters and set them on the bar so we can all reach them.

"So, anyway," I say after putting the plate between the three of us, "he said some things that really made me think."

Rock pops one whole quarter sandwich into his mouth and gives me a thumbs-up.

"Like what?" Kristen asks, grabbing a sandwich and taking a healthy bite. I, on the other hand, only manage to pick at the crust of one of the sandwiches. My conversation with Jay has my stomach in knots.

But watching Rock with his elbows on the table, attention focused entirely on what I'm saying, I realize I can't come right out and ask Kristen what I'd intended. The last thing I want to do is point out more of my faults with him standing right in front of me.

I shake my head. "Never mind."

Kristen slaps her hands on the counter. "Would you please just tell me already?"

Of course she won't drop it. "It was nothing," I hedge.

"Come on, Sarah," Rock says. "It's just us."

When I look up, Kristen and Rock are sitting side by side, but not touching. Both of them are watching me way too closely, letting me know there's no way I'm getting out of this. "It was just something he said."

"Which was . . . ," Kristen leads.

"Stupid, really. That's what it was."

"Am I going to have to pull this out of you, word by word?" she asks. "Because you know I will."

Rock leans back in his stool, arms folded across his chest. The look on his face is very overprotective, like a big brother would have. And I guess I should think it's sweet he wants to protect me, but the heat spreading across my chest is anything but sisterly love.

"For starters, he *claims* he's had some sort of crush on me since we started high school."

"I knew it!" Kristen squeals.

"Calm down," I grumble. "First of all, you most certainly did *not* know it. If you had, you would've been pushing me to go out with him for years. Secondly, I'd bet anything he's just saying that. There's no way Jay, or any guy for that matter, has been eyeballing me for four years. How could I not notice that?"

Kristen pouts from her seat, angry I haven't jumped on the "Jay for Boyfriend" campaign.

Rock leans forward, stretching his arms across the counter that separates us. "How can you possibly think a guy wouldn't jump at the chance to go out with you?"

I narrow my eyes at him. "History."

Kristen speaks quietly, eyes on the counter. "You really haven't given anyone a chance."

The sandwich I'd been holding drops onto the plate. Of all the things I expected Kristen to say, that wasn't it. "Come again?"

"Think about it," she says.

"I've thought about it plenty." When I hear how defensive my voice sounds, I cringe.

Rock raises an eyebrow at me, as if he has a clue what it's like to be teased his entire life about something he can't control.

"What did you say when he told you that?" Kristen asks, finally meeting my eyes again.

"I didn't have time to say much of anything," I say. "He jumped right into his second beef with me, rambling on about how I push people away, but that's just more lunacy. I mean, sure, there are people I totally avoid, but that's only because they've given me grief over my nose."

Kristen doesn't say anything, just looks at me.

"He also asked me out again," I say.

"Again?" Rock asks.

Smiling, Kristen laughs. "That's because he really likes you. What did you say?"

"No, of course."

"You should be careful, Sarah," Kristen says. "You can only say no so many times before he'll quit asking."

Rock puts his brown eyes on me. "Is that what you want, Sarah?"

Staring at Rock, I want to scream out how much I want him and only him. I want to tell him that no one will ever come close to measuring up now that I've met him. That I've poured my heart into the Facebook and e-mail messages and how can he not see that it's me? But I wisely keep those words tucked safely inside my throbbing head.

I ignore him, facing Kristen instead. "*You* never answered *my* question. Do I push people away?"

Kristen's smile falls. "The answer's complicated," she says.

My heart stutters when I realize she isn't going to disagree with Jay. "So you think I *do* push people away? Do you have any idea how ridiculous that sounds?"

Kristen leans across the counter to get closer to me. "No one knows you better than I do, right?"

I nod in answer; there's absolutely no one who knows me better than Kristen.

"Well, I think Jay might have a teeny tiny point," she says, fingers held up with a minuscule space between them.

"And what would that point be?"

"Look, it's not your fault. It's human nature to protect yourself from getting hurt. But you know as well as I do that Jay Thomas isn't out to break your heart."

"Come on, Kristen. Think about it. It's not like guys are

burning up the cell-phone satellites calling me every night, so how could I possibly push them away?"

"But you've spent years putting up a wall to keep people from hurting you. You can be so defensive. Maybe it's intimidating."

Part of me is completely proud of that statement (not that I believe it's entirely true). After all the wisecracks about my monstrous nose, I think it's only fair that they're a tad bit intimidated by me. The best defense is a strong offense, right? Didn't someone famous say that?

"I wish you knew how amazing you are," Kristen says quietly.

I smile, so thankful I have her.

Rock pulls himself forward and rests his tan arms on the counter between us. "So the question stands."

"What question?" I ask, lost.

"Do you want Jay to quit asking you out?"

I take a deep breath and close my eyes. I try to picture myself with Jay, and it's not an entirely unpleasant sight. We're both blond, attractive, and have great smiles. Even so, I just can't force the image to come together in a convincing way.

When I close my eyes, there's only one guy.

Slowly opening my eyes, I look at Rock. I'd give anything to know what he's thinking. Or maybe not. I definitely don't need to hear how much he pities me.

I nod my head, then pull my eyes from Rock, afraid I might jump over the counter and start kissing him as if I have a right to. "Yeah. I want Jay to quit asking me out."

"Omigod," Kristen says, fully exasperated. "Ron White's right. You can't fix stupid."

"Ron White?" Rock asks, shaking his head like he's just woken up from a dream.

"Please tell me you know who he is. He's one of the comedians from Blue Collar Comedy. Tell me you've heard of him." Kristen's got one hand on her hip, disbelieving.

"Oh yeah. Sure," he mumbles.

I put the plate in the dishwasher along with the skillet and spatula. "Don't forget that's in there," I tell Kristen.

"You're leaving?" she whines. You'd think she wasn't sitting here with the hottest guy to ever walk through her front door.

"Yeah, I shouldn't have barged in." I smile at Kristen, then at Rock. "You kids have fun."

Before I can grab my backpack, Rock lifts it from the counter and puts it on his shoulder. "I'll help you out," he says.

"Thanks," I say, reaching for my backpack. "But I've been lugging that thing around for years. I can manage."

"Don't bother arguing with him," Kristen says, slurping the last of my drink. "He's totally hardwired to be a gentleman."

I shrug. "See you in the morning, Kris."

"Okay," she says with a sad smile, like she's about to face judgment from God himself. If Rock weren't standing six inches from me, I'd drill her about it. The only thing she should be feeling right now is pure joy. She's beautiful and has Rock in her back pocket. What could possibly be wrong?

Rock puts his hand on my back and guides me from the

kitchen, keeping me from asking Kristen what's bothering her. But I don't fight him and promise myself I'll call her later tonight.

Once outside, Rock walks next to me with a lazy comfort and ease that's about as charming as it gets. I swear, the guy doesn't have a single insecure bone in his body.

He opens the back door to my car and drops the backpack on the seat. "So," he says.

"Guess I'll see you tomorrow," I say, wondering why the air around us has suddenly become thick, making it hard to breathe.

He leans closer to me, eyes on mine. "Sure you're okay?" he asks.

"Why wouldn't I be?" I practically whisper. Honest to God, his face is a foot from mine and I'm struck positively stupid.

"You seemed pretty upset about Jay," he says, eyes still fastened on mine in that completely unnerving way he has. If I didn't know any better, I'd think the guy could see every thought racing through my mind.

I shake my head. "I'm fine. Thanks, though. And thanks for the help with my bag." Which, I realize, I never used. Thank God he never asked why I needed it.

"Sarah—" Rock says, then stops.

I wait for a second, and when he doesn't say anything more, I ask, "Yes?"

"We're friends, right?"

Friends.

The word slams into me like I've run headfirst into a brick wall.

"Of course," I tell him. Friends is all we'll ever be.

"And you trust me?" he asks, still close enough for me to enjoy the heat from his body.

"Of course," I repeat, worried he's about to unload the brutal facts on me. Something to the tune of "If you'd just fix your nose . . ."

He rocks back on his heels, eyes shifting to the ground between us. "The truth is . . . I think you're incredible."

Incredible? Did he just call me . . . *incredible*? I stand frozen with my heart doing Olympic-worthy gymnastics in my chest.

He raises his eyes back to mine, a grin on his face. "You don't believe me."

I won't even let my brain go where my heart has already raced. I won't let myself believe Rock actually likes me. *Really* likes me. And so what if he did? My loyalty would still be to Kristen. It always will be.

I smile back at him. "I think you're a really good friend. A protective friend. And I really appreciate it, but—"

Rock shakes his head, impatient. "That's not what I meant."

"Then I'm lost," I tell him.

He clears his throat abruptly. "I don't know how to—" he begins, then stops when Kristen opens the front door.

"Y'all lose something out here?" she calls from the front door.

I close my eyes, willing him to finish what he was going to say. It could have been anything.

I don't know how to read braille.

I don't know how to crochet.

I don't know how to tell you I love you.

I nearly laugh out loud at the last thought. Geez, maybe I *do* need to get out of town this weekend.

Even when I look around him to answer her, Rock doesn't move, keeps his eyes on me. "Just chatting," I call back with a small wave.

"So . . . ," I say, wishing he'd tell me what he's thinking. There's something going on in that gorgeous head of his and I'm dying to know what it is.

I open the car door and slide into my seat. *Say something, Rock.*

Rock holds the door, an unreadable expression on his face. "Good to see you tonight, Sarah."

"You, too, Rock." I pull the door from his grip and close it, but roll the window down, giving him one last chance to say whatever was on his mind.

His eyes are on me; his unspoken words are hanging between us. "See you around," he says quietly, then taps the hood twice before he turns around and strides back up the sidewalk, where Kristen's waiting for him.

Even as I pull from the curb, I can still feel Rock's eyes following me, his unspoken words now question marks swirling around in my head.

There is no cosmetic for beauty like happiness.
—MARGUERITE GARDINER BLESSINGTON

Chapter Eighteen

When I get home, I find Mom reading on the couch, feet enjoying the warm vibrating water of her favorite footbath. It's one of those supercool ones that keep the water hot for hours.

"Hi, sweetie," she calls over her shoulder as I enter the living room. The smell of lavender fills the room. Those aromatherapy hippies know what they're talking about. The scent immediately loosens the tightness in my shoulders.

I drop my backpack and purse on the floor and fall into the cushion next to her.

"Tough day?" she asks, dropping the book and grabbing my hand for a squeeze.

"Confusing," I tell her.

"Feel like talking about it?"

One of my favorite things about Mom is that she doesn't force me to talk about anything. It's always my choice. And nine times out of ten, I talk. A lot.

I tell her about the things Jay told me, right down to the impossible-to-believe story that he'd had a crush on me for years.

When I finish telling her how our conversation ended, Mom stays quiet. Her eyes are soft, intense, like she's choosing her approach with me very carefully.

"Just say it," I tell her.

"Sweet Sarah," she says. "How can you be so smart and still so . . ."

"So *what*?" I demand when she pauses.

"So unaware," she finishes.

I stare at her like she's officially lost her mind. Because, let's be honest, she has. "I know you're still reeling from the whole Jen thing, but that's *your* issue. Don't make it mine."

"This has absolutely nothing to do with Jen," she says, spitting out Jen's name like she just swallowed a huge gulp of sour milk, "and everything to do with you."

I laugh out loud because if I don't, I seriously might cry. Why can't she just support me 100 percent, no questions asked?

She reaches down and turns off the footbath, then dries her feet with the towel in her lap. She sits cross-legged on the cushion, facing me. "Sarah, I know it's hard to believe, but I was your age once. And I had the same nose you do."

"You keep saying that, but I've never seen a single picture that proves it." Trust me. I've done plenty of digging for old pictures and yearbooks over the years, but I've never unearthed a single photo of her pre-rhinoplasty.

"That's because I moved heaven and earth to erase that part of my life. I didn't have the confidence you have. There wasn't a single day I wanted to keep that nose. Not one single day."

None of this is new information. Mom's told me a million times about how she saved every penny from her after-school job at the mall for three years to get her nose job. It's clear she felt imprisoned by her nose.

"You hated your nose. Got it. What does that have to do with *me*?" I ask.

Mom sighs a deep breath, then speaks so quietly I have to strain to hear her. "Has it ever occurred to you that maybe you're not as tough as you let others believe?"

"Who said I was tough?" I ask, matching her tone. As much as I don't want to have this conversation, something deep in my gut tells me I need to. Not that Mom would ever let me escape now. She's got me and we both know it.

Mom smiles, a sad little smile, one full of regret. "You've been fighting to prove that since the day you were born, Sarah."

I shake my head. "Whatever."

"It's true, you know. Even when you were a toddler, you kept everyone at a distance. It was like you didn't need anyone."

I focus on the intricate pattern of the rug, doing my best to block her out and failing.

"Sarah, look at me."

I cut my eyes her direction. "What?"

"I think Jay may be on to something."

"I can't believe you're taking his side. You don't even know him!" Aren't mothers supposed to be on your side, no matter what?

Mom laughs, like I said something freaking hilarious.

213

"There are no sides here, Sarah. And if there were, you can bet I'd be on yours. All I'm saying is that there's some truth to what Jay said."

I fold my arms over my chest, glaring at her and feeling completely betrayed.

"When was the last time you hung out with someone besides Kristen?" she asks.

Narrowing my eyes, I shrug. "What does that have to do with anything? It's not like there are people out there just dying to be my friend."

"How can you be so sure?" she pushes.

"The barrage of never-ending big-nose one-liners and snickering when I walk by is a pretty good indicator. Trust me, if someone said hello or even smiled my direction, I'd notice."

"So how is it you missed Jay's crush on you?"

The truth is, I've been asking myself the same question all afternoon. In a sea of sarcasm, how could I have missed Jay's laugh, his warmth?

Would it have mattered?

"The answer's pretty obvious, if you ask me," Mom says slowly.

When I stay silent, she pulls my chin with her soft hand so that we're facing each other.

"Sarah Burke, I love you. I think you are the most amazing person I've ever known and I thank God every single day for you."

I refuse to give her any leeway. "You have to say that. You're my mom."

She giggles, sounding and looking more like a college girl than a middle-aged woman. "I guess all moms feel that way," she concedes. "But I wasn't finished."

I hold up my hands. "My bad. Please go on."

"Sarah, you're a difficult person to get to know. You're adamant about keeping your nose the way it is, but you won't look strangers in the eyes. You keep your eyes down and heart closed to new people who might want to get to know you better. I understand how you feel, and I know kids have teased you over the years. I'm not saying that's easy to deal with or that it's fair. It's all a matter of *you* accepting who you are, Sarah. Everyone else around you has already done that, and those that haven't don't matter anyway."

"You've been reading Dr. Phil again, haven't you?" I say, the sting of her words burning my eyes.

She playfully slaps at my hand. "Don't let your nose keep you from life. Don't let it limit the people who get to know you and love you the way I do. I guess that's why I always pushed the nose job on you . . . I was never as strong, as independent, as you. I craved approval and attention from everyone else. I guess a part of me still does. But you don't, Sarah. You're perfect just as you are."

I look at my mom, a sinfully proportionate, stunning, successful woman. "It's hard to imagine you with a single flaw," I say.

"Trust me, I still have flaws. Lots of them."

"Yeah, right. Tell that to the million people that watch you on the news every night."

"You know," she says, "I've been thinking about what happened between you and Jen at the station. I'm really proud of you for sticking up for me. For us."

"You would have done the same thing," I say, feeling a rush of warmth on my face.

"Not at your age, I wouldn't have. If I'd been the seventeen-year-old standing in that doorway, overhearing those ludicrous rumors, I'd have run and hid. But you've got more guts than I ever had. That's why you don't need a nose job to make you feel complete, worthy."

I stare at Mom, wondering if she could possibly be right. Could someone really love me with my nose exactly the way it is?

More importantly, can I learn to love myself? Nose and all?

✦ ✦ ✦

More than once, I thank God that I don't have to go to school and face Rock so soon after that weird exchange at my car. With the weekend as a buffer, I'm pretty sure I can pretend nothing ever happened. And I've been blessedly spared a call from Jay.

But I'm not nearly as lucky in steering clear of Kristen. Not that I'm really trying to avoid her, but I'm not quite ready to face her when I'm still muddling through my feelings about my life and who I am. And I definitely don't need to hear the details of her latest date with him. When she shows up unannounced Sunday morning, I'm still in my pajamas, working at the computer on an article for journalism.

"God, don't you ever get tired of doing homework?" she

complains, stretching out on my unmade bed, stroking Ringo curled up on my pillow. He rolls onto his back for more attention, which Kristen freely gives him.

"Doesn't matter if I'm tired of it. It still has to be done," I tell her, smiling at her predictability.

"So you and Rock say," she mumbles, arm thrown over her eyes.

"Something on your mind?" I ask, glancing back at the half-written article on the computer screen, wishing I could finish it.

"Yep," she says, eyes still covered.

"Care to share?" I ask.

She pulls her arm from her eyes and rolls onto her stomach to face me. "It's Rock."

I brace myself for the play-by-play of her date. I press my lips together tightly and let her take over the conversation.

"So we get to this place called the Chocolate Bar in Montrose. It's totally amazing—chocolate everywhere! The smell alone is enough to give you a caffeine buzz."

"Definitely sounds like my kind of place," I say, picking at my fingernails.

"It was the most romantic setting for a date," she says, eyes drifting to some faraway place in her mind, like she's watching the night unfold in her head.

"That's so great," I say, stopping myself from hurrying along this little stroll down memory lane.

"But then the poetry reading began."

I smile, sure that Kristen's about to reiterate her reasons for hating poetry. Always at the top of that list is, "Who talks like that, anyway?" which is followed closely by, "Why are poets so cryptic? Just say what you mean already!"

But she shocks me with the look in her eyes that tells me things aren't so sunny in paradise. "That's when things started falling apart," she says.

I hop off the chair and sit down on the bed close to her. "I'm sure it's not that bad."

"It was awful," she moans, sitting up so we're side by side on the edge of the bed. "I kept trying to make comments about the poetry but he just kept smiling and laughing, like I was purposely saying things to make him laugh." I reach around Kristen and pull her in for a little hug, and she drops her head to my shoulder.

She sighs deeply. "I think I'm going to break up with him."

My heart skids to a screeching halt, and the air is sucked out of my lungs.

Kristen raises her head and studies me. "Don't look so surprised," she says. "You had to know this would happen. It's not like I can keep up the facade without you around. That was painfully evident last night."

"But it's *Rock*," I say, feeling oddly conflicted. Thrilled, on the one hand, that he'll actually be free, but terrified on the other. Because now there will be nothing to stop me from telling him how I feel. Aside from my burgeoning insecurity and the fact that twenty-four hours ago he was dating my best friend, of course.

"Exactly. He'll understand when I tell him." She nods her head resolutely. "Right?"

"When you tell him what?" I ask, already sensing what's coming next.

"About the e-mail and Facebook messages you wrote. I mean, if he hadn't figured it out already, he has to know after last night."

"You swore you'd never tell, Kristen. Besides, he probably just thinks you were being cute," I suggest in desperation.

"There is nothing cute about being dumb. Not in Rock's book, anyway. Besides, it's too much work."

I stare at her, infuriated that she'd ever consider telling him I'd written the letters. "It's too much work for *you*?" I nearly scream. "*I'm* the one who wrote those letters. *I'm* the one who spent hours on Facebook thinking up believable replies and coming up with questions to keep the conversation going. You can't tell him, Kristen. You swore you wouldn't tell him."

"Breathe," she tells me. "You've seriously got to relax. Geez."

"You. Promised." My voice is lower, but still shaky.

"I won't tell him *you* wrote the letters, just that I had someone else write them for me. I owe him the truth."

"Since when did you grow a conscience?" I ask her, instantly regretting it when I see the hurt cloud her eyes. I hug her tight. "I'm sorry. You know I didn't mean that."

She pulls away, looking at me through watery eyes. "That was way below the belt."

I nod. I'm not too proud to admit when I'm wrong. And that was way wrong.

Kristen stands, walks to my computer, and scans the

article on the screen. "Do you have any idea how long it'd take me to write something like this?" she asks, pointing at the screen.

I shrug. "We all have different talents."

"If that's true," she whispers, "what are mine?"

My eyes are glued to hers. In all the years we've known each other, I've never heard her talk like this.

"You are about a million times more talented than I ever thought about being," I tell her.

She shakes her head emphatically. "I dare you to name just one real talent. Something you can say I'm really good at."

I hold up my index finger. "First of all, you're a social genius. You know exactly how to make everyone feel comfortable at a party."

"That's a personality trait. What can I *do* that's special?" she asks, pleading me with her eyes to come up with something. Anything.

"You always know exactly what to wear and when. If it wasn't for you, I'd have spent the last four years in jeans, faded T-shirts, and flip-flops."

"Anyone can learn how to dress from watching *What Not to Wear* and reading a fashion magazine."

"You've got mad math skills, Kris. I've never seen anyone calculate equations in their head the way you do. I've got to be honest. It's a little bizarre." I end with a little chuckle to let her know I'm teasing.

She cocks her head to the side, studying me, then breaking into a small grin. "Well, it's not writing, but I guess it's something."

I nod, unsure of what to say next, not sure I should say anything at all. All I know is, for the first time since I met Kristen Gallagher ten years ago, I realize she's as insecure as I am.

Two weeks ago, I would have laughed if you'd called either one of us insecure. As sure as I'm sitting here, watching my best friend grapple with self-doubt, I know it's true.

Underneath our bravado, we're the same.

Beauty is the pilot of the young soul.
—RALPH WALDO EMERSON

Chapter Nineteen

By the time Monday morning rolls around, I've thoroughly obsessed over Kristen's pending breakup with Rock. I only know she plans to break it off "when it feels right," which, in Kristen's world, could be today. Or June.

I don't have a clue what to expect when I enter journalism for third period that morning. Is he going to be heartbroken if Kristen's already broken it off with him? Is he going to act all weird about the conversation he and I had outside Kristen's house? The whole thing has my gut in knots. But there's no way I'm skipping. I've been busting my butt on an article that's due today and has a shot at being put in the school paper. You can never have too many published articles to make your college applications shine.

I stride into class just as the bell rings and take a deep breath to prepare myself for what I might find. But, like always, Kristen and Rock are in their usual seats, chatting and smiling.

The only thing different about today is they aren't glued to each other like two ticks. I take my seat in the next aisle with a questioning look to Kristen.

"Hi, Sarah," Rock says, full smile telling me what I need to know. She hasn't broken up with him. Yet. There's a part of me that wants to warn him because I don't want to see him get hurt. But I would never do that to Kristen. Being Kristen's bestie is not for the weak.

I smile back at Rock and give a stupid little wave. Like there's some huge distance separating us and he can't hear me speak. Geez. But I'm so grateful that he isn't acting all weirded out from Friday that I totally let myself off the hook.

"Do anything special this weekend? Make it to Salado with your mom?" he asks.

I pause a beat before answering, momentarily lost. "Mom got called to work." I'm getting entirely too good at lying. I hold up the paper I've written. "So I just wrote."

"Write, write, write," Kristen says sadly, shaking her head. "I swear, that's all you do."

I give her a pointed look to let her know she's not being funny. I mean, she's totally pulling my chain because she knows I'd kill her for telling Rock I'd written all those messages. But still. It's enough to get on my very last frazzled nerve.

"All work and no play," Rock teases.

"Very funny," I snap back, maybe a little more fiercely than I'd intended.

"You should have joined us for the poetry reading," he

tells me. "You would have loved it. There was a guy there who did the most amazing Lord Byron reading."

"Oh yeah," Kristen agrees halfheartedly. "Amazing."

Rock playfully shoves her. "This one's a regular comedian. She had the one-liners coming all night."

I can't stop myself from chuckling, knowing the one-liners he's referring to. I give the girl props for even trying. Talk about being out of your element.

"Yeah, you never know what she's going to say," I agree.

One look at Kristen and I know she's done.

Done with the charade of being something she's not, and done with Rock.

✦ ✦ ✦

I spend my lunch period scarfing some seriously stale peanut-butter crackers and chasing down the school counselor. I desperately need him to write a letter of recommendation to accompany my scholarship application. If I get the station scholarship Jen told me about, I can at least say Mom and I got one good thing out of her.

It's not until I'm crawling into bed at ten thirty that I hear from Kristen. When my cell phone rings, this time playing the oldie "Brick House," I know it's her.

"I did it," she breathes into the phone.

"Rock?" I ask, clarifying before I let my emotions run rampant.

"Yep," she says, typically stoic. She's always like this after a breakup, like it was inevitable that every single relationship has to end.

"What'd you say? How'd he take it?" I ask in a rush.

"Um, I told him the truth." Her words are so matter-of-fact I nearly come through the phone to strangle her.

"You *told* him?"

"Chill, Sarah. I didn't tell him *that*. I just said we didn't have that much in common."

"What'd he say?" I ask quietly, barely recognizing the tightness in my voice. I try to focus on our conversation, try to ignore the obnoxious thudding in my chest that she'd totally hear if she was in the room with me. But it's impossible to concentrate. All I can think about is Rock.

"He took it pretty well, actually. It was weird, you know? Kind of like he expected it."

"He didn't ask a bunch of questions?" I ask, stunned he didn't put up a heroic fight to keep her. And if I'm honest, I'm just the tiniest bit happy he didn't. Okay, I'm a lot happy he didn't.

"No, not really. I explained to him that I'd had help writing the e-mails and Facebook messages. But I didn't say who," she says quickly.

But I can't relax because everything's changed. Even though I hated Kristen dating Rock, at least then I knew what to expect. I knew exactly where I stood. I was comfortable, in a constant, heartbroken kind of way. Now everything is different. I'm not even sure he'll still be friends with me now that he and Kristen have broken up. It suddenly dawns on me that because Kristen's broken up with Rock, I kind of have, too. Now I'll only see him in class.

Unless I'm willing to do something about it.

Unless I'm brave enough to tell him exactly how I feel.

"So I'm back to riding to school with you. I'll drive this week, okay?" she says, breaking my reverie.

"Sure," I mumble. "Don't be late."

+ + +

When Kristen picks me up ten minutes late, I'm too tired to muster any real indignation. After hanging up with her last night, I tossed and turned for hours. I'm not sure how much sleep I actually got, but it wasn't nearly enough.

"Oh, man. Are you getting sick?" she asks, looking way too put together for someone who just broke up with her boyfriend. I've probably lost more sleep over this than she has.

I attempt to hold back a yawn. "No, I'm not getting sick. Couldn't sleep last night."

In the blink of an eye, Kristen launches into a long-winded story about the last time she couldn't sleep and all the different things she'd tried.

"Do you know what finally worked?" she asks, a rhetorical question if there ever was one, which is a good thing, since I'm only half listening to her rambling.

Without waiting for my reply, she answers. "Warm milk! Sounds totally gross, I know, and way too *Little House on the Prairie* or something but it worked like a charm."

She pulls into a parking space that appears to be a country mile from the school's entrance. "Could we be any farther from the door?" she complains.

I stop myself from telling her this is the kind of parking spot you get when you're late.

We part ways after getting our tardy slips from the office. When I stumble into trig, I have to face an irritated Mr. Marshall.

But it hardly even hits my radar because I'm 100 percent focused on what I'm going to do—or not do—about Rock.

✦ ✦ ✦

It seems like an eternity, but I finally make it to journalism. I'm surprised to find Rock sitting in his usual seat in front of Kristen. The two of them are talking like normal and I instantly relax. I don't know what I was expecting, but Kristen's breakups usually come with some fireworks or, at the very least, desperate pleas from the jilted boyfriend for her to give him another shot. More than once, I've been responsible for relaying those desperate requests to Kristen.

"There she is," Rock says, like he's been waiting for me all day. As if.

"Am I late?" I ask, eyebrow raised in that cocky way my mother loathes.

Rock looks at Kristen, who's way too happy for my liking, and then back at me. "You don't know?" he asks.

I shrug, playing dumb and hoping he doesn't want to talk about his breakup with my best friend. "Know what?"

Kristen can't help herself and rudely interrupts Rock before he can get another word out.

"You know your article? The one you turned in yesterday? Mrs. Freel is entering it into some sort of statewide contest."

"What?" I practically scream. "When? How do you know?"

227

Rock smiles. "They said it on this morning's announcements."

I glare at Kristen. "Which we missed because we were late."

"Sorry," she says, hands in the air like we're in some lame bank robbery and the villain's told her to "Stick 'em up!"

"But I thought the assignment was for the newspaper," I say.

"It was," Mrs. Freel says, surprising me when she pops into my peripheral vision. She walks closer, a warm smile on her face. "But I fell in love with your paper, Sarah. I hope you don't mind that I entered your paper without discussing it with you first. We have until tonight at five o'clock to withdraw your entry if that's what you choose. But I really think you've got a shot, and there's a two-thousand-dollar scholarship for the winner."

I blink my eyes quickly, flattered and utterly shocked. "Don't apologize. I'm happy you entered it. Thank you," I tell her, beaming like a fool.

"Excellent," she says with a proud smile. "I was hoping you'd say that."

"Tell me about your paper," Rock says as Mrs. Freel walks away to close the door and begin class.

"It was an essay on loyalty. The difference between our loyalties to our family, our friends, our school, our country, and what I think is important." I sit back in my seat. "Wow."

"Very cool, Sarah," he says, giving me an encouraging smile and that killer wink.

"I don't know why you're so surprised," Kristen says. "You could write a novel about paint drying and make it sound intriguing and unforgettable. Look what you did for me."

My cloud of elation evaporates when Rock narrows his eyes in question. Judging from the look on Kristen's face, she knows she's blown it. And instead of covering up her mistake like she normally does, she sits frozen, eyes wide.

"You?" Rock asks.

"I tutor Kristen," I lie, eyeballing Kristen and willing her to back me up.

"She's tried her best to help me with my writing, but I'm hopeless. She still keeps trying, though. Won't take no for an answer." Kristen stops her rambling when I clear my throat.

I nod at her explanation, hoping Rock buys the absurd lie. "Stubborn to a fault."

He looks at Kristen, then back at me as he swings his legs back under his desk and faces the front of the classroom.

Call it instinct, woman's intuition, or sixth sense, but I can practically see the cogs in Rock's brain spinning.

+ + +

I'm quick to bolt from the classroom when journalism ends and escape to the restroom, where I can avoid Rock. Two weeks ago, I'd have given anything for extra time with him, but I can't make myself face him. Not when there's a lie between us, especially one as big as this.

Of course, I can't ditch class (being such a good student is seriously beginning to affect my social life), so I slink down the hallway and into Jacobi's class. I'm relieved when I find Rock isn't there, but I know I can't evade him forever. I'll be doing good to escape a scathing interrogation (which I completely deserve) in the next fifty minutes.

Rock jogs into class seconds before the bell rings, a seriousness on his face that instantly sets my nerves on edge. More alarming is the way he eyes me as he walks to his seat behind mine. He sits without smiling, the first time he's ever done that.

And I can feel it in my bones.

He knows.

As Jacobi begins class, I wish for the first time that he'd just shut up and let me think. Not that I'll be able to justify what I did to Rock, but if I could just have ten minutes to formulate some sort of half-assed excuse, I could at least face him.

"Don't run out after class," Rock whispers into my hair, sending a chill of dread down my back. "We need to talk."

Wholly incapable of replying, I give one sharp nod to indicate I heard him and then spend the next fifteen minutes racking my brain. What am I going to tell Rock? I'm so lost in my own thoughts I'm surprised when everyone in class begins shifting their desks to set up for partner work. Great. Just my luck.

I know it's childish, but I squeeze my eyes shut and pray for some way out of this. Of course there isn't, which is obvious when Rock spins my desk around to face him with me still in it. Normally, I'd be turned on by such an awesome display of strength but, right now, I'm closer to puking than swooning.

"I can't believe it was *you*," Rock whispers furiously, leaning across his desk so that we're mere inches apart.

"What was me?" I ask, attempting to play dumb. Normally, I detest it when girls do that, but I'm totally backed into a corner.

Rock's eyes narrow and dread races through me. This is bad. Really bad. "Give me a damn break. You think I didn't figure it out after Kristen's little slip? I know you wrote those e-mails and Facebook messages for her, and you know what's really pathetic? That I didn't figure it out before. How could I have missed it? It's so freaking obvious. Especially after the comment about people noticing your nose before your eyes." He shakes his head in disgust, as much as with himself as at me. "But I believed her. I believed *you*."

"I'm sorry, Rock. It was just one of those crazy ideas that kind of got away from us. But I promise you, I stopped when I knew the two of you were getting serious. Once I got to know you, I just couldn't keep it up."

Rock leans back in his seat, tense arms folded across his chest. Jacobi drops a sheet of paper with our assignment between us, unaware that my life is completely falling apart right here, right now. I look down at the paper, but I can't make out the words through the tears threatening to spill over. I squeeze my eyes tight to fight them back.

"I'm sorry, Rock. I don't know what else to say."

"I thought you were my friend, that I could trust you," he says quietly, looking at me with such disapproval that it takes my breath away.

"I *am* your friend."

He shakes his head, then gives a sarcastic laugh. "Could've fooled me."

Beauty is an experience, nothing else. It is not a fixed pattern or an arrangement of features. It is something felt, a glow or a communicated sense of fineness. What ails us is that our sense of beauty is so bruised and blunted, we miss all the best.

—D. H. LAWRENCE

Chapter Twenty

If I thought watching Kristen and Rock together was the worst possible misery, I was dead wrong. Because the last two weeks without Rock talking, joking, and encouraging me has shown me just how utterly wretched life can really be. Not once has he even made eye contact with me, each day growing more distant, literally and figuratively.

He no longer sits next to me and Kristen at lunch or in journalism. And he quickly found a new seat in Jacobi's class, leaving me to partner with Alyssa Dunwoody.

And no matter how many times I replay the events that led to losing Rock, I can't figure out a way to fix it. The one thing I understand is exactly where I went wrong and why. It's not something I can really talk about with Kristen, either.

There has been one shining light in the shambles of the past two weeks: my essay on loyalty made it to the top five (which seems totally preposterous given the way I've treated

Rock). The best part is that being a finalist guarantees me a five-hundred-dollar scholarship.

At the very least, I'm enjoying the extra attention from Mrs. Freel, who makes a point to visit with me each day and has offered to write a letter of recommendation for my college and scholarship applications.

"Sarah," Mrs. Freel calls to me as class ends, exactly sixteen days since I last spoke to Rock.

"Yes?" I answer, making my way to her desk and waving good-bye to Kristen as she leaves the room.

"I received an e-mail today regarding your entry in the scholarship contest," she says, face and eyes neutral.

My heart drums in my chest. "I thought the results weren't due back for another two weeks."

"They aren't. But they are allowing every finalist to revisit their essay and make changes. The revision window is small; you only have forty-eight hours. If you'd like to do that, make sure you have it to me no later than the end of the day tomorrow."

I chew on my bottom lip, considering the opportunity to edit my essay. "Do you think I should?"

Mrs. Freel smiles at me. "Only you can decide that. Trust your gut, Sarah. You've got top-notch instincts."

I nod, wishing she'd decide for me. I mean, I'm dealing with enough right now. What if I change it and it totally sucks?

"Okay, thanks," I say, then leave the room with my head more crowded than ever.

+ + +

At nine fifteen that night, I'm sitting at my computer, hands resting on the keyboard, mindlessly tapping the keys as I think. I stare at the existing essay on the screen, the one I was writing the night Kristen told me she was breaking up with Rock.

The one that's earned me a spot in the top five.

Loyalty.

The very word evokes strong emotion. By definition, it means a feeling of devotion, duty, or attachment to someone or something. It's considered the core foundation of all successful relationships, both personal and professional.

There are few things in life that better define a person than this honorable virtue. It isn't an easy one to possess. It takes practice and dedication. Sometimes, we even have to fall off the wagon, so to speak, before we realize its importance in our life.

There are varying types of loyalty that we all possess to some degree: loyalty to our family, our friends, our school, and our country. It means standing up for the people and things you believe in when others fight to bring them down. Sometimes, it means putting yourself in an unpopular position to defend the honor of those closest to you.

But if we fail to practice it, fail to value its place in our life, where would we be?

We'd be a world full of unhappy families, defined by strife and distrust.

We'd have no friends to rely on, forced to live out each day on our own.

We'd be a defenseless country, with no one to fight in the name of freedom.

And what kind of life would that be?

Without much thinking, I start typing, letting the words flow from my heart (instead of my head) in a rush, without editing, without revision. Everything that's happened to me over the past three months spills onto the screen, the good, the bad, and the really shameful.

Forty-five minutes later, I print the regurgitation of my rambling thoughts and read the revised essay.

The satisfaction that comes from spilling your guts, even if it's on the computer screen, is beyond description. It's all right there: the brutal facts. There's nowhere to hide, no one to blame but yourself.

I'm not at all convinced this paper is as good as my last one, but it's honest. It's real. And it's something I'm proud of. Before I can change my mind, I e-mail it to Mrs. Freel and ask her to submit my revision.

I shut down my computer, turn out the lights, and crawl into bed with Ringo curled up next to me.

For the first time in weeks, I slip off to sleep in mere seconds.

+ + +

When I wake up the following morning, there's a purpose in my steps, a fire in my eyes, and I feel more alive than I have in a long time. I don't even stare at the mirror and fixate on my nose.

It's part of who I am; take it or leave it.

Even when Kristen arrives five minutes late, I greet her with a smile, happy to have her in my life. On my terms from now on. I consider telling her about my revised paper, but I dismiss the thought when she starts gossiping about Jay and how he asked another girl to homecoming.

Kristen rolls her eyes. "For someone who was so love struck, he sure got over you fast."

I know she doesn't say it to hurt me, and I'm not upset. If anything, she's furious with Jay for not fighting harder for me.

"If it's what makes him happy, then I'm cool." I smile in her direction as she shoots me a look of total disbelief.

"Oh my God," she groans, "what am I going to do with you?"

I laugh, happy to have our easy banter back, knowing my happiness doesn't rest on Kristen's and wondering why it took me so long to figure that out.

✦ ✦ ✦

Friday afternoon, I arrive at Jacobi's class early, skipping the trip to my locker. When I walk inside, there's only one other person there.

Rock.

Sitting in his new seat on the other side of the room, he looks so different from the vision that runs through my head every night. There's no smile, no spark in his eyes.

I take a deep breath and walk closer, sitting in the seat in front of him and turning around to face him.

He looks up, an unreadable expression on his face.

I clear my throat before speaking. "Can we talk for a minute?"

He shrugs. "It's a free country," he says.

"Yeah," I mumble. Geez, he's not exactly making this easy on me, is he? But I guess I don't deserve a break.

"So," I say, "I've done a lot of thinking about what happened. You have every right to be angry with me. I'm angry with myself for doing it."

Rock looks up at me, eyes still hard, no trace of the warmth I was hoping to find. He stares at me, silent.

"I guess I thought I was being a good friend to Kristen. She was desperate to get your attention, you know? To prove to you that she was smart. And she knew you were into things she wasn't. The ironic thing about all of this is that every word I wrote was written from the heart."

"Whose heart?" Rock asks in a low growl. "Were they even your words or did you copy them out of some lame romance novel? What am I supposed to believe?"

"Give me some credit. Of course they were my words. It started with a letter Kristen had written and I just . . . spiced it up a little."

"So they were Kristen's words," he says, disbelieving.

I shake my head, ignoring the kids filtering into the classroom, knowing I'm nearly out of time. "Not exactly."

Rock shakes his head. "Yeah, that really clears it up."

Someone taps me on the shoulder and I look around to see Rock's new lit partner standing impatiently behind me. I stand up and move next to Rock's desk.

"Can we finish this at lunch?" I ask, stopping myself short of begging him.

Rock looks up at me, then nods. "Meet me on the front steps."

"I'll be there," I whisper, fighting the smile that threatens to spread across my face. It's not like I expect Rock to fall in love with me; too much has happened for that to be a possibility. But if I can just convince him how sorry I am and why I was so misguided, maybe we can at least be friends.

+ + +

I grab a salad from the cafeteria and give Kristen my usual excuse for missing lunch.

"Scholarship application," I say as I walk past our table. "See you after school."

She rolls her eyes and waves, watching me race out of the cafeteria. What's most surprising is that I don't even consider how she'd feel about me talking to Rock. It's time to be true to myself.

When I shove through the double doors to the front steps, I run into a wall of black leather and silver studs. The bikers. Or wannabe bikers, anyway. Most of them aren't even old enough to have a license, but the way they dress and behave, you'd think they were the newest Hells Angels inductees.

I stand frozen in place, wishing I had Kristen here to back me up. But this is the new me, I remind myself. The confident, self-reliant me.

Some creep snickers from the corner. "Holy shit. Did your parents lose a bet with God?"

The familiar tension crawls up my neck. I glare through the crowd of losers, daring them to say another word to my face, but they avoid making eye contact. Cowards.

A hand grabs mine and pulls me through the crowd and down the stairs.

"Punks," Rock grumbles. He drops my hand the second we're on the stairs.

I follow Rock to a small patch of grass and sit next to him. Now that I'm here and finally have his attention, I'm speechless. I mean, how far do I really want to take this?

"Are you going to say something?" he asks, opening my salad and picking at the carrots. It's an innocent act, but it resembles the easy way we used to be with each other and gives me the courage to open up.

"You want to know whose words were in those messages," I say. It's more of a statement than a question but he nods his head in answer, opening the small plastic bag of stale croutons and popping them into his mouth like they're pieces of popcorn.

"Well, it started as Kristen's words. She'd written a letter that needed some work so I rewrote it. What you saw in that e-mail were my words, but . . ."

For the first time since coming outside, Rock looks at me.

Really looks at me. Like he's trying to determine if I'm telling the truth, if he can trust me.

"But what?" he asks.

I sigh deeply, wishing I didn't have to say this out loud, but knowing I do. It's the only way I'll ever know for sure.

Swallowing what little pride I have left, I whisper, "It's how I felt, how I still feel."

Rock pulls his knees up and rests his arms on top, looking out into the parking lot, eyes squinting in the sunlight.

I keep my eyes on him, waiting for some sign that will tell me what to expect next.

"What am I supposed to say to that, Sarah?" he asks quietly, eyes still straight ahead.

I shrug, even though he isn't looking at me. "I don't know, Rock. I guess that's something you'll have to decide."

He nods, then turns his face to me. "Why'd you do it? If you felt that way about me, why would you help Kristen?"

I lean back on my hands. "Because it's what I do," I say.

"Lie?" he asks with a streak of sarcasm so sharp I feel like he's slapped me.

But how can I be angry with him for calling me out? "Until recently, I would have done anything to make Kristen happy. Even lie."

"Until recently," he repeats.

"I finally figured out I have to do what's right for me first."

Rock nods, then clears his throat. "Wish you'd figured that out sooner."

"Me, too," I agree. "For what it's worth, I hope you can

241

accept my apology and we can be friends again. That's what I miss most of all."

He twists the lid off his bottled water and takes a swig. "Me, too," he says, then pops to his feet and leaves me sitting on the grass alone.

Beauty of whatever kind, in its supreme development,
invariably excites the sensitive soul to tears.

—EDGAR ALLAN POE

Chapter Twenty-one

Weeks pass with nothing more than quick, meaningless glances between Rock and me. I refocus on my schoolwork, the one place I always do well, and try to forget how monumentally I failed with Rock.

Houston finally gets its first cold front of the season one week before Thanksgiving. That same cool morning, Mrs. Freel calls me to the front of the room as class begins.

I walk to the front of the room and stand next to her, hands shoved into my hoodie. I focus 100 percent of my attention on Kristen. I haven't locked eyes with Rock since the day I spilled my guts and then watched him walk away. The last thing I need is to watch him enjoy the embarrassment of whatever's about to happen next.

It's easy to ignore him when he's taken to sitting in the seat closest to the door. The way he bolts in and out of class, it's like just being near me is enough to make him sick. If I wasn't so insulted, it'd be funny.

Mrs. Freel puts her coffee cup on her desk. "Sarah, I received a phone call last night from the head of the scholarship committee. It seems they've made their decision."

And she's telling me here? Now? In front of the entire class?

I turn my eyes to her, try to read her expression, but it's stone-cold serious. My stomach plummets and my mouth goes dry.

"They were very impressed with your writing," she says, a small smile creeping onto her face. "Really impressed."

Someone hollers "Hell to the yeah!" and others follow with whistles and catcalls, which is totally flattering in a really embarrassing kind of way.

"So impressed, in fact," she says, "they decided to award you first place in the scholarship contest."

The class erupts into clapping and whistling. Mrs. Freel wraps her arms around my neck and brings me in for a huge hug that forces all the air out of my lungs. I pull back and smile, gasping for breath.

"I thought it'd be nice if you read the essay aloud to the class," she says when everyone finally quiets down.

Panic invades every cell of my body, ratcheting my heart rate to a dangerous level. Can a seventeen-year-old die of a stroke?

The essay is about Rock.

And Kristen.

How can I possibly read it aloud? There's no way.

I shake my head at Mrs. Freel. "That's okay. They don't want to hear it."

"Don't be so humble, Sarah. You've earned this award." Mrs. Freel is looking to the class for encouragement, which promptly riles up my classmates.

The class chants, "Sar-ah! Sar-ah! Sar-ah!" It's not like they really want to hear what I've written. I know these kids—they just want out of whatever assignment Mrs. Freel has planned for the day.

"Your fans are calling," Mrs. Freel says just loud enough for me to hear. "Show them what real writing sounds like."

She pats my back for support, then hands me the paper filled with my words, my gut-deep feelings spread across the page.

I look at Kristen, who's in full chant, standing on the seat of her chair as she pumps her fist into the air with each syllable of my name. It's hard not to laugh. She's absolutely the best friend ever. It's not her fault the reading of my paper's going to qualify as my life's most embarrassing moment.

I close my eyes and take a deep breath as Mrs. Freel shushes the class with a finger over her red lips.

"Whenever you're ready," she says, taking a few steps back, leaving me totally on my own.

Clearing my throat, I hold up the paper and begin reading.

"*Loyalty.*

"*The very word evokes strong emotion. By definition, it means a feeling of devotion, duty, or attachment to someone or something. It's considered the core foundation of all successful relationships, both personal and professional.*

"But what about loyalty to ourselves?

"*In* Hamlet, *Shakespeare penned a well-known but often forsaken phrase: To thine own self be true.*

"*Is it true that we owe ourselves the same loyalty we pledge to others? How do we reconcile that belief with our loyalty to others, especially when it comes at the cost of our own happiness?*

"*I've recently learned something very profound: loyalty to others can be a weakness if you don't know how to balance it with loyalty to yourself, to your own ideals and goals.*

"*This wasn't a lesson I learned easily. It came after weeks of refusing to follow my own instincts in order to make another person happy.*

"*But it's funny what you can convince yourself to do in the name of loyalty, in the name of friendship.*"

I stop to catch my breath, swallowing loudly. Fighting the tears is a losing battle and I don't dare look up at Kristen. One look at her and I'll be toast. Before I lose my nerve, I take a deep breath and read on.

"*When my best friend asked me to do something I knew was wrong, I did it anyway. Now I wonder why I would sacrifice my own self-interest for hers. And it all boils down to that one seven-letter word.*

"*Loyalty.*

"*Clearly, I was misguided in my devotion to our friendship. I can rationalize it all, of course. Maybe I didn't believe I really stood a chance to get what I wanted, so it was easy to ignore my own desires. Maybe I was just scared. Scared of rejection, embarrassment, and, worst of all, abandonment.*

"Still, what haunts me most about my failure to do what was right for me is that I denied myself the opportunity to be truly happy. Since my life-altering mistake was revealed, I haven't felt the same peace and joy in my heart that was there before.

"Honestly, there's a part of me that believes I've earned the misery I'm living through right now.

"As a seventeen-year-old senior at Northwest High School, I'm proud to say I'm a good friend, maybe even a great friend. But I know now exactly how far I'll go for that friendship and vow to show myself the same loyalty I've given others. I deserve a place on my list of priorities. I've learned that my own happiness is as important as anyone else's and loyalty to myself is paramount.

"Thank you, Shakespeare, for the words that now guide my heart, my every decision.

"To myself I will be true."

When I finish, you can hear a pin drop in the classroom. Even Kristen, who's still standing in her chair, is frozen in place. The look on her face says it all.

She gets it.

She knows I was attracted to Rock, but that I helped her anyway.

She knows exactly what I sacrificed. For her.

She hops off her chair and races to the front of the room, pulling me into a hug so fierce, so tight, I'm not sure I have the strength to pull away.

"I love you, Sarah," she mumbles into my hair. "I'm so sorry I didn't know."

I laugh, my body's automatic defense to that telltale burning in my eyes. "It's okay," I say, patting her back.

"Okay, girls," Mrs. Freel says, chuckling.

"Kiss and make up," a crude boy's voice calls out from the back of the room.

"That's enough," Mrs. Freel says in response before turning her attention back to me and Kristen. "Kristen, please sit down."

Reluctantly, Kristen pulls away from me, then walks back to her seat.

"Congratulations, Sarah," Mrs. Freel says, taking the paper from my shaking hands. "We're all very proud of you."

I smile back at her. "Thanks."

Walking back to my desk, I can feel Rock's eyes on me and it takes every ounce of restraint to keep my eyes on my desk. There was nothing in that essay I hadn't already told him, so he can't be surprised.

But right or wrong, I'm aching to know what he thinks just the same.

✦ ✦ ✦

Sitting at our table in the cafeteria, I wait for Kristen, wondering if her emotions have shifted from regret to anger. Not that I think anger would be appropriate, but it's been my experience that's how most people react when they feel guilty. It's always easier to blame someone else than to own up to your mistakes.

When she finally sits down across from me, she smiles, and I immediately relax.

"Are we okay?" I ask timidly.

"Of course we are," she says, sprinkling two packets of Parmesan cheese on her oversized slice of pepperoni pizza. "I just can't believe that's how you felt and you never said anything."

"I didn't even question it until Rock found out."

"Well, that's the first thing you've got to get settled," she says, mouth full.

"What?" I ask, confused.

"Rock."

I shake my head quickly. "I've tried to talk to him about it, but I didn't get very far."

"Then I'll talk to him for you," she offers.

"Absolutely not," I say, pointing my finger at her. "Don't even think about it. Do you understand?"

"Okay, okay," she says. "Geez, just trying to help."

"I know you are," I say. "But this is between me and Rock."

"I should have known it was you," she says quietly.

"What do you mean?"

"When we were at the Chocolate Bar at that poetry reading, he kept looking around the room. I asked him who he was looking for and he just shrugged and shook his head."

"What does that have to do with me?" I ask, stomach churning at the thought of Rock looking for me. I don't dare let myself believe it's true.

"Well, isn't it obvious? He was looking for you. He'd spent

the entire drive to Montrose talking about the poetry the two of you had discussed in class."

"Whatever," I say, doing my best to blow her off. The last thing I need is to get my hopes up. After all, he's made it painfully clear he's done with me now. So whatever he felt three months ago is long gone.

"Think what you want, but I'm telling you Rock feels the same way. When have I been wrong about guys?"

I stare at Kristen for a long moment. "It's too late," I say quietly, as much to myself as to her.

"Girl," Kristen says with her usual spunk. "It's never too late."

✦ ✦ ✦

After taking Kristen home, I stop at the store for groceries. Knowing Mom's doing the ten o'clock doesn't keep me from planning a full spread for the night: chicken Parmesan with ziti and a Caesar salad. I need the distraction and Mom can heat it up when she gets home.

When I finally turn onto my street, it's close to five and I'm shocked to see a familiar truck parked in the driveway.

Rock's truck.

Instinctively, I slow down and actually consider pulling a U-turn.

But it's Rock.

Isn't this what I wanted?

I force myself to keep my foot on the gas and pull into the driveway beside his truck. By the time I hop out and reach in the backseat for the groceries, he's beside me.

"Let me get it," he says gruffly, almost like he's irritated.

"Thanks." I move out of his way and let him grab the two bags.

"I was hoping we could talk," he says after closing the car door.

I nod, afraid to trust my voice. Instead, I walk across the lawn to the front door.

"Where've you been?" he asks. Maybe it's a little over the top for him to ask, but a part of me is thrilled he even cares.

"School, Kristen's house, then the store. It's not like I was expecting you to be here," I say.

"Yeah, I know," he says from behind me. I open the door and let him follow me to the kitchen.

"You can just put those there," I tell him, pointing to the kitchen counter.

He carefully puts the bags down, then looks around the comfortable kitchen, eyes stopping on the wall of pictures.

"Want something to drink?" I ask.

"No, thanks," he says.

I grab a bottled water from the fridge and walk to the living room, then sit on one side of the oversized couch.

"Is this a picture of you and your mom in Hawaii? The trip you wrote about?" he asks.

I look at the picture of us on Diamond Head. "Yes," I tell him. "We spent two days in Honolulu, then flew to Kauai, which is the island I told you about."

Instead of answering, he nods, continuing his study of the pictures.

"What's up?" I ask, desperately needing him to get to the point. Twenty minutes of chitchat is liable to send me over the edge.

He walks away from the pictures and sits down next to me, turning so we're face-to-face. Being this close to him after so long has me breathing like I just ran the stadium bleachers. Twice. So much for playing it cool.

"Do you remember the day you told me about writing the e-mails and Facebook messages for Kristen?" he asks, eyes back to their usual soft warmth.

"Of course I remember." I don't bother telling him that's the day everything went to hell.

"Right," he says, obviously embarrassed. Like I could have possibly forgotten that day.

He wipes his hands on his jeans. "I've done a lot of thinking about what you said that day. I'll admit I was mad when I figured it out. But I was as mad at myself as I was at you or Kristen. Maybe I was more embarrassed than anything. I'm usually smart enough to pick up on that kind of thing, but you got me."

A small grin creeps onto my face. "What can I say? I'm good."

He chuckles. "Obviously," he says. "But the more I thought about it, the more I realized you were only doing what you thought was right. And even though I understood that, I still couldn't let you off the hook."

"So why are you here?" I ask, fighting the urge to toss my lunch.

"There was something you wrote in that essay," he says. "It was the part where you said you didn't believe you deserved what you wanted. When you said you thought there wasn't a chance for you to have what you desired."

I nod, mortified to hear my own thoughts coming from his lips.

"Is that true?" he asks, eyes narrowed as he lowers his voice to a whisper.

Taking a deep breath, I lean back into the cushion. "It took you and Kristen a grand total of sixty seconds to hook up. Why would I think I stood a chance with you?"

"I've actually been thinking about what attracted me to Kristen. It really wasn't the way she looked, it was more about the attention she gave me. New kid in a big school getting lots of attention from someone like Kristen . . . it's pretty flattering," he says.

So much for him sweeping me off my feet. "That's understandable."

"But later, what *kept* me dating her was the way she put her feelings into words. I've never known anyone who could write like that. Then I found out they weren't her words at all. They were yours. *You* were the one who was touching me bone deep and I didn't even realize it."

"There's more to me than my writing skills," I tell him.

"You think the most important part of who you are is this," Rock says, horrifying me when he lightly taps my nose. "But it's not. It's just one beautiful part of who you are."

I shake my head, knowing that of all the attractive parts of me, my nose is definitely not one of them.

"Sarah Burke, you have a big nose," he says, smiling.

I slap his shoulder. "Thanks a lot. You're free to go now," I say, planting my feet on the ground and lifting my stunned body off the couch.

He pulls my hand until I'm sitting right next to him, and he doesn't let me go. He keeps my hand tucked securely in his. "I love your nose, Sarah. And what I feel for you . . ." He stops, eyes on our hands locked together. "I don't know where this will go, but I want a shot."

There's no use fighting the stinging tears. I've waited my entire life to hear someone say these very words and it's not just any guy. It's Rock.

I finally find my voice. "A shot at what?"

"At us," he says definitively. "I think we deserve a chance."

Nodding, I look him in the eyes, totally losing myself in the moment and committing it to memory. I don't want to forget one single second of what's happening.

"Is that a yes?" he asks, uncharacteristically timid.

"It's a yes," I whisper back, not trusting myself to speak normally, knowing I'm about ten seconds from bawling right here in front of him.

Rock keeps his hand in mine, then pulls me closer. I swear, we're moving in slow motion when he leans down and lightly touches his lips to mine. There isn't even the slightest hesitation as he moves in closer and closer to my face, no accidental bump of my nose, no sudden change of heart.

It's a total movie moment. The only thing missing is the swell of the orchestra in the background.

And I feel like the luckiest girl in the entire world.

Because sometimes the best gift you can give yourself is a second chance.

Acknowledgments

None of this would be happening if not for the incomparable Holly Root, agent extraordinaire. You were able to see *Flawless* on the shelves long before anyone else and patiently answered my endless questions about what to expect in a highly unpredictable industry. I totally want to be you when I grow up.

To Caroline Abbey at Bloomsbury . . . thank you for taking a chance on a debut author and for making my first revision experience a dream. You somehow made every suggestion sound like a compliment. Without fail, seeing your name in my in-box makes me smile. To Donna Mark, the supremely talented cover designer . . . seeing the cover was like seeing my children for the first time. Thank you for bringing *Flawless* to life.

Caleb and Laney . . . there is nothing in life worth having that doesn't include you.

Mom . . . if I had one wish, I'd ask to have you with me

again. I miss you more than I ever thought possible. See you on the other side.

My life would be incomplete without the love and support of my family, especially my dad, Ron Christopher, and my sisters, Karen Watson and Mary Gail McCarty. And I have to add my best friends, Pam Brown and Michelle Hall. The roller coaster that became my life was bearable only because you were by my side. Kiss-kiss!

To all the people who read, critiqued, loved, and cheered for *Flawless* that weren't related to me . . . Laura Gompertz, Joann Robisheaux, Linda Kryzwicki, Tera Lynn Childs, Sharie Kohler, Diane Holmes, Kay Cassidy, and Mary Lindsey. Thank you for believing in me when I'd given up on myself. I am proud to call you friends.

A big shout-out to West Houston RWA and Young Adult RWA . . . my friends, publishing experts, marketing geniuses, and cheerleaders. Your place in my life is as necessary as air.

To Kathryn Lorenzen and the River Rats . . . never forget . . . the best revenge is living well!

Janet Evanovich . . . you are a genius! After I'd read everything you'd published, I grabbed *How I Write* simply because it had your name on it. That book changed my life forever.

To the students who keep me young(ish) year after year . . . the promise of your laughter gets me out of bed each day. Life's short . . . live large!

Finally . . . for anyone who isn't sure if karma actually exists, the past fifteen months of my life prove that it does. Pay it forward . . . your day is coming.

LARA CHAPMAN grew up loving school, especially new school supplies (who doesn't love the smell of new crayons?). She loved school so much, in fact, she tried to make a career out of it, but after an extended stay in college prompted her father to announce she couldn't be a professional student, she finally declared a major and graduated with her teaching certificate. Since then, she's been teaching various subjects at the intermediate school level—currently, fifth grade language arts—and loving every second of it. She has served as the editor of numerous professional journals and organization newsletters, distributed both in print and electronically. Lara lives with her family in Dime Box, Texas (it's as small as it sounds), where she reads and writes daily. She's rarely—if ever—found without her laptop and iPhone.

www.larachapman.com